PRAISE FOR **Now Is Not the Time to Panic**

"Wilson's fiction will have you laughing so much that you're not prepared for the gut punch that follows. . . . *Now Is Not the Time to Panic* is the heartfelt culmination of many years (and many pages) spent probing the tension between the urge to make a mark on the world and the costs of doing so—and the push-pull between art's disorienting and generative powers. . . . Go read Wilson's books. You'll discover one-of-a-kind worlds opening up."

—*Atlantic*

"*Now Is Not the Time to Panic* is a quirky, complicated story about the power of words and art, and the importance of adolescent friendships." —*Time* (A MUST-READ BOOK OF 2022)

"A charming coming-of-age novel brimming with nostalgia."

—*People*

"Wilson has developed a story that is a precise capture of adolescence and of two vibrant teens whose everyday dilemmas, weaknesses, and triumphs are utterly endearing. . . . Crisp dialogue and a zipping story line." —*Booklist* (STARRED REVIEW)

"This is a wildly funny, wonderfully sincere—and a little bit devastating—story of art, our limitless past, future nostalgia, and all those perfectly imperfect ways we continually come of age. Kevin Wilson's books are so full of heart. They're utterly indelible." —Courtney Summers, *Washington Post*

"It's the kind of book your cool English literature teacher would recommend when you showed an interest in writing, the type of coming-of-age story that would have been equally destined for a banned-books list *and* a summer reading list." —*Vulture*

"A novel about creativity and childhood that seems as though its author has been mulling over since his own youth. It bears the markers of Wilson's style—cleverly cute without tipping over into saccharine territory. . . . Though the book has an earnest heart, it's colored by Wilson's appealingly offbeat prose, so that even the most straightforward coming-of-age moments have a funky freshness."
—*Vogue*

"Kevin Wilson once again deploys his customary humorous, off-center storytelling to artfully delve into deeper matters. . . . His deceptively transparent prose, with a touch of humor, a dash of satire, and a good bit of insight, carries the reader to a humane and satisfying conclusion."
—*BookPage* (starred review)

"The latest glorious novel from Kevin Wilson. *Now Is Not the Time to Panic* is about oddballs and misfits; it's about art and how the making of art turns what's weird about you into what's magical about you."
—Oprah Daily

"Wilson's latest novel shows us again that he is at the top of his game, infusing this coming-of-age tale with his trademark sharp wit and deep understanding of love and the uncertainty that comes with fading youth."
—*Chicago Review of Books*

"The Tennessee native spins tales so droll and clever and casually surreal, it feels less like reading than falling in with a delightfully subversive new friend."
—*Entertainment Weekly*

"A seductive, highly imaginative story that testifies to the transformative power of art."
—Associated Press

"A bighearted novel." —*Vanity Fair*

"What Wilson so eloquently captures is that unique time in one's life when one small gesture of artistic self-expression—a madcap sentence about living on the fringes and embracing your eccentricities, come what may—really does have the power to change the world, or at least your perception of it."

—*San Francisco Chronicle*

"Wilson's most emotionally nuanced and profoundly empathetic novel yet. . . . Highly recommended as a sincere, sometimes brutal, but always sturdy study of the burden of both art and adolescence and a wonderfully evocative treatise on how we imprint ourselves on the world and learn to survive in that tumultuous wake." —*Library Journal*

"Wilson occupies a unique niche in literature. He is a master of creating indelibly peculiar characters with odd passions and traits. . . . All those peccadilloes have a purpose, though. They give shape to the characters' humanity and fuel narrative arcs that tell evocative tragicomic stories about family, friendship, love, and art that end on a note of cautious optimism. And, honestly, isn't that the best we can reasonably hope for in life?"

—*Atlanta Journal-Constitution*

"A book destined to become a cult classic, if not just a classic, period. . . . *Now Is Not the Time to Panic* departs from the comic surrealism of Wilson's previous novels . . . in favor of a kind of sepia-toned realism that never ceases to entertain. Frankie and Zeke are wholly original characters, their lives painful and true, and while this is a novel you can read in a single sitting, it is best devoured slowly, a treat for the heart and mind."

—*USA Today* (four stars)

Now Is Not the Time to Panic

ALSO BY KEVIN WILSON

Tunneling to the Center of the Earth

The Family Fang

Perfect Little World

Baby, You're Gonna Be Mine

Nothing to See Here

NOW IS NOT the TIME to PANIC

A Novel

KEVIN WILSON

ecco
An Imprint of HarperCollins*Publishers*

This is a work of fiction. Names, characters, places, and incidents are products of the author's imagination or are used fictitiously and are not to be construed as real. Any resemblance to actual events, locales, organizations, or persons, living or dead, is entirely coincidental.

A hardcover edition of this book was published in 2022 by Ecco, an imprint of HarperCollins Publishers.

FIRST ECCO PAPERBACK EDITION PUBLISHED 2023

Designed by Paula Russell Szafranski

Library of Congress Cataloging-in-Publication Data has been applied for.

ISBN 978-0-06-291351-7 (pbk.)

23 24 25 26 27 LBC 5 4 3 2 1

In memory of Eric Matthew Hailey

(1973-2020)

MAZZY BROWER

I ANSWERED THE PHONE, AND THERE WAS A WOMAN'S VOICE on the other end, a voice that I didn't recognize. "Is this Frances Budge?" she asked, and I was certain it was a telemarketer, because nobody called me Frances. In the living room, my seven-year-old daughter had made her own set of drums, including a tin plate for a cymbal, so it was loud as hell in the house, with this ting-bang-ting-ting-bang rhythm she had going on. I said, "I'm sorry, but I'm not interested," and started to hang up, but the woman, understanding that I was done with her, tried her best to pull me in.

"The edge is a shantytown filled with gold seekers," she said, her voice rising in pitch, and I froze. I nearly dropped the phone. And together, in harmony, we both completed the phrase, "We are fugitives, and the law is skinny with hunger for us."

"So you know it," the woman said.

"I've heard it before, yeah, of course," I said, already trying to run away. I could feel the world spinning around me. *Oh shit, oh shit, oh shit, fuck, no* in my head, a kind of spiraling madness, because, you know, it had been so long ago. Because, I guess, I'd let myself think that no one would ever find out. But she'd found me. And I was already trying to figure out how to get lost again, to stay lost.

"I'm writing an article for the *New Yorker*," she told me. "My name is Mazzy Brower, and I'm an art critic. I'm writing about the Coalfield Panic of 1996."

"Okay," I said.

"Mom!" my daughter Junie was shouting. "Listen! Listen to me! Listen! It's 'Wipe Out,' right? Doesn't this sound just like 'Wipe Out'? Mom? Listen!"

"And I think you made it happen," the woman said, treading carefully. Her voice sounded nice, honest.

"You think I made it?" I said, almost laughing, but it was true. I *had* made it. Not just me, but I was part of it. Me and one other person.

"I'm almost one hundred percent certain that it was you," Mazzy Brower said.

"Oh god," I said, and I realized I was saying it out loud. My daughter was banging away. I felt dizzy. There was a pizza in the oven. My husband was finally fixing the latch on a window in our bedroom, which we'd been meaning to fix for four solid months. Our life, which was so boring and normal, was still happening. Right at this moment, as everything was changing, it was like my life didn't know it yet. It didn't know to just stop, to freeze, because nothing was going to be the same. Let the pizza burn. Forget about that stupid, shitty latch on the window. Pack up your stuff. Let's get the hell out of here. Let's burn down the house and start over. For a split second, I thought maybe just *I* could get out of here and start over.

"Was it you?" the reporter asked. Why had I picked up the phone?

"Yes," I finally said, and I could feel my whole body being pulled through time. "Yes, it was me."

"Just you?" she asked.

"It's complicated," I replied. My daughter was now standing beside me, pulling on the back of my shirt. "Mama?" she asked. "Who are you talking to?"

"Just a friend," I told her.

"Let me talk to her," Junie said, the most confident person I'd ever known, holding out her hand for the phone.

"I have to go," I said to Mazzy.

"Can we meet?"

"No," I said.

"Can I call you back?"

"Sorry, no," I told her. And before she could say anything else, I hung up the phone.

I started to pace around the kitchen, trying to remember every word of the conversation, what I'd said to this woman. But Junie hates pacing, hates when she sees me go inside myself, and so she started tugging on my pants.

"What's your friend's name?" Junie asked.

"What? Oh . . . Mazzy," I said.

"Mazzy sounds like an imaginary friend," Junie said.

"Maybe she is," I told her. "I'm not entirely sure that she's real."

"You're so weird, Mama," Junie said, smiling. And then, like it didn't matter at all, because she'd already forgotten, she said, "Listen to me play these crazy drums!"

There was still time. I sat on the couch. And I watched my daughter, with two wooden spoons in her hands, absolutely whale away on anything that was around her. And my heart was pounding in my chest. It was over, I kept thinking. It was all over. And it was beginning. It was just beginning.

PART I

The Edge Is a Shantytown Filled with Gold Seekers

SUMMER 1996

One

AT THE COALFIELD PUBLIC POOL, THEY WOULD BLOW A WHISTLE and everybody had to get out of the water, and we'd all stand there, hopping on one foot and then the other because the concrete was so damn hot, burning the bottoms of our feet. And some lifeguard, barely older than I was, sixteen, looking like the bad guy in a teen movie, blond and buff and absolutely never going to save you if you were drowning, would wheel out a greased watermelon. There was a three-inch layer of Vaseline, which made the watermelon shiny, almost like it was turning from a solid into a liquid. And the lifeguard and one of his evil twins, maybe with crazier muscles and a scuzzy mustache, would dump this watermelon into the water and then push it to the middle of the pool.

And when they blew their whistles, the point was to jump into the water, and then whoever could get the watermelon to the edge of the pool would win it. You had to team up, really, to reasonably expect to win the thing, and so the game would turn into a kind of gang war, boys basically beating the shit out of each other, this watermelon slipping and sliding away from them, almost an afterthought. By the time it made it to the edge, the watermelon was covered in gouges from fingernails, pieces of the red meat of the fruit spilling out of it, pretty much inedible to anyone except the person who'd won it. I was smart enough to stay away, though it made me mad that no girls ever really took part, like we were too delicate for things like this. But the only time I'd tried, when I was twelve, some old man with a snake tattoo on his arm elbowed me in the face and nearly knocked out my front teeth.

The triplets, my brothers, were perfect for the greased watermelon contest, because they were eighteen and already giant. They were nearly feral, possessing a kind of strength that wasn't just physical but a psychosis that made them impervious to pain, which they tested out on each other all the time. But they didn't take part, either, because they used this time while everyone else was hypnotized by the watermelon to steal money and snacks from unattended bags.

I was standing there, my feet blistering, wondering why I didn't just go lie down on my towel and wait for the time when I could safely wade back into the pool and . . . what, exactly? Just keep wading around and around, so you could never quite tell that I was alone? I hated the pool, but the A/C had blown out back home and it would be another day before it was fixed. I'd held out for two straight days, sweating and miserable, but finally hopped in the van with my brothers that morning. Honestly, if I had to be here, I wanted to see the fight over this thing. I wanted to hear the shouts and curses. I wanted to see violence done in the name of fun.

A boy was watching me from across the pool. I could see him, skinny and twitchy, probably about my age, and every single time I caught him looking at me, he'd smile this goofy smile and then stare down at the water, the sun reflecting off of it so brightly that it was blinding. I lost sight of him. Any second now, the lifeguards were going to blow their whistles. And then I felt somebody touch my elbow, which for some reason felt really intimate and weird, someone's fingers on my rough, bony elbow. I whirled around, and it was the boy, his eyes black, his hair black, his teeth bright white and painfully crooked. "Hey," he said, and I pulled my arm away from him.

"Don't touch people that don't like being touched," I told him. He held up his hands in surrender, looking shy all of a sudden. Who touches a girl's elbow and then gets shy?

"Sorry," he said. "I'm sorry. I'm new. I just moved here. I don't know anybody. I've been watching you. It looks like you don't know anybody, either."

"I know everyone," I said, gesturing to the entire congregation of poolgoers. "I know them all. I just don't *like* them."

He nodded. He understood. "Will you help me get this watermelon?" he asked.

"Me?" I asked, confused.

"You and me," he said. "I think we can do it."

"Okay, sure," I said, nodding, smiling.

"All right," he said, his face brightening. "What's your name?" he asked me.

"Frankie," I told him.

"Cool. I like girls who have boys' names," he told me, like he was the most open-minded boy who had ever lived.

"Frankie isn't a boy's name. It's unisex."

"My name is Zeke," he told me.

"Zeke?" I said.

"Ezekiel," he explained. "It's biblical. But it's my middle name. I'm trying it out this summer. Just to see how it sounds."

I was looking at him. He wasn't handsome; all of his features were too big, cartoonish. But I wasn't pretty, either. I had a really plain face. I convinced myself, at the right angle, that even though I was plain, it was temporary and soon I'd be pretty. I told myself that I definitely wasn't ugly. My brothers, however, said I was ugly. Whatever. I cared so much, but I put a lot of effort into not caring. I was punk rock. Maybe it was better to be ugly if the alternative was to be plain.

The whistle blew, and we were just staring at each other, but then he said, "C'mon. We can do this!" and he jumped right into the pool. I did not jump into the pool. I just stood there. I smirked, watched him bob in the water. And he looked so hurt. It made me feel real shitty. Finally, he shrugged and started splashing toward the commotion, toward that roiling mass of teenage boys, all fighting over something so stupid, for fun.

Zeke tried two or three times, but he kept getting roughly tossed aside, dunked under the water, and he'd come up gasping, coughing, looking so lost out there on his own. But he kept climbing over people, trying to get his hands on the watermelon, which was so slippery that no one could really control it. And then somebody kicked him accidentally in the mouth and I saw that his lip was busted. It was bleeding, dripping into the pool, but the lifeguards did not give a shit.

I don't think they were even watching. And Zeke just jumped back into the crowd, and I started to get worried. I knew something bad would happen to someone this clueless.

Before I could think about it, I was running over to my brother Andrew, who had, like, seven bags of snack-size Doritos, and I told him that I needed his help. Right then, Brian came over, a wad of damp dollar bills in his fist. "C'mon, Andrew," he said, completely ignoring me. "We don't have all day."

"I need help," I said, and by this point, Charlie had come over, wondering what was going on. "I need you to help this boy get the watermelon," I told all three of them.

"Fuck no," Charlie said. "No way."

"Please?" I asked them.

"Sorry, Frankie," Andrew told me, and they started to run off, but I shouted, "I'll give you twenty dollars!"

"Twenty bucks?" Brian asked. "No shit?"

"Twenty bucks," I said.

"And what do we do now?"

"See that nerdy kid in the water? With the busted lip?" I told them. They all nodded. "Help him get the watermelon," I said. It was pretty simple, but they kept staring at the watermelon.

"You in love with him?" Charlie asked me, grinning.

"I don't know," I said. "I think I feel sorry for him."

"Yikes," Andrew said, grimacing, like I was cursed. "Fine. We'll do it." And my brothers dropped all the stuff they were carrying and ran to the edge of the pool, cannonballing into the water. Andrew grabbed Zeke like a rag doll and basically carried him toward the watermelon while Brian and Charlie cleared a path using their elbows, the ferocity of their actions overwhelming the other kids, who had been wrestling over the watermelon for long enough that they were starting to tire out. When they got possession of the watermelon, a sorry-looking sight, Andrew threw Zeke onto it, and the triplets pushed him to the edge of the water, Zeke's mouth dripping blood onto the Vaseline. And then it was over. Zeke had won.

The lifeguards blew their whistles, and the other kids acted like they didn't care. Their chests and arms were glistening with the grease, and it wasn't coming off in the water, but they just started splashing around, waiting for the girls to get back into the pool, the kids in their floaties, the dads with their beer guts and sad tattoos.

I walked over to the edge of the pool, where Zeke was trying to catch his breath. My brothers had already left, gone to find new ways to distract themselves.

"You did it," I said.

"Who were those boys?" he asked, so confused.

"My brothers," I told him.

"You did this?" he asked me, and I nodded. We both laughed.

"Your mouth is bleeding," I told him, but he didn't seem to care. We both stared at the watermelon, which looked like a horror movie, so many half-moon marks digging into the green rind, that greasy, disgusting film all over it.

"Will you eat this with me?" he asked.

"You're going to fucking eat that?" I asked.

"We're going to eat it," he said, smiling. And we did. We really did. It was so good.

Two

IT WAS SUMMER, WHICH MEANT THAT NOTHING WAS HAPPENING. It was insanely hot, making it hard to care about anything other than eating Popsicles. My house was empty; my mom was working, my dad was in Milwaukee with his new family, and the triplets were all flipping burgers at different fast-food restaurants. I'd wander the house, listening to music on my headphones, never changing out of my pajamas. I was supposed to get a job, but I hadn't filled out any of the applications. I was fine with just keeping up my babysitting gigs. My mom, who loved me so much and was so tired, gave up, let me have the house to myself, and at first I was happy for the silence, but soon it began to feel oppressive, like the walls knew I was the only person there and could shrink down to hold me in place.

I wasn't looking for a friend or anything like that. I was bored. And Zeke, this new boy who seemed stunned to find himself in this dinky little town, was something that could occupy my time.

Two days after we'd first met at the public pool, after I gave him a little piece of paper with my address on it, Zeke rode his bike over to my house. He had on an oversize black Road Warriors T-shirt, two angry wrestlers, their faces painted, weird shoulder pads. My brothers loved these dudes, too. I couldn't imagine people who seemed more different than Zeke and my brothers, but if you were a boy, there were just things you loved, I guess.

"Hey," he said, smiling. "I live, like, four blocks away."

I just shrugged, unsure of what to do now that he was here.

"Thanks for inviting me," he said. I shrugged again. What was wrong with my tongue? Why did it feel so fuzzy?

"This town is weird," he said. "It's like a bomb was dropped on it, and you guys are just getting back to normal."

"It's pretty boring," I finally said, and my jaws ached with the effort.

"It's always better to be bored with someone else," he offered. I gestured for him to follow me inside, into the air-conditioning.

I didn't know exactly what to do with him, but I wanted it to be clear that we weren't going to have sex in my empty house. I had been nervous over the past two days, worrying what I was or was not getting myself into, all the things that I did not yet want to do. I needed Zeke to know that it wasn't that kind of thing, so we just sat on the sofa and watched horror movies on VHS, eating Pop-Tarts, which felt so far away from what I thought sex might be that it seemed safe.

I was trying to put off talking for as long as possible, until it became inevitable. By then, I thought, I'd have something interesting to tell him.

"Do you like it here?" Zeke asked me while I was taking out one tape and trying to put in another. And now we had to talk. I guessed I was okay with this.

"It's fine," I said, crouched over the VHS machine. And it *was*, honestly. What would I do in a city? Go dancing? Eat a fifty-dollar steak at some fancy restaurant? Well, I mean, maybe go to a museum. That would be fun. But I was sixteen. I lived inside of myself way more than I lived inside of this town.

"But," he said, pressing me, "what do you do for fun?"

"This," I said, frustrated, holding up a copy of *Fright Night*. What did he want from me? Did I have to prove to him that I was cool, that I didn't belong in Coalfield? "Why?" I finally asked, turning it back on him. "Where did you come from that's so great?"

"Memphis," he said. "And it's not so great, really. But, you know, there's some okay stuff. Memphis Chicks baseball games. Mall of Memphis, you can ice-skate there. Audubon Park."

"Well, okay, that does sound pretty cool. Ice-skating would be cool."

"But," he said, smiling, "here we are."

"Why did you move here?" I asked him.

"I didn't have any say in it. It's messed up." He kind of looked at me for a few seconds, like he was trying to decide what he would and would not tell me. And this intrigued me, that his story required editing. I got up off the floor and sat next to him on the sofa.

"My dad's been having an affair," he told me. "I guess he's been having a few of them, because one of the women found out about the other one."

"Oh, god," I said.

"Yeah, and she called our house to rat him out, but I answered the phone. And she told me about how he was really a bad guy and was treating her wrong, and that I needed to divorce him and then get that other lady to stop seeing him, and only then would she think about staying with him, and I was like, 'Ma'am, I'm his son,' and she said, 'Oh, honey, you have such a high voice,' and I hung up."

"Your voice isn't that high," I offered.

"Well, on the phone I try to be super polite, so my voice is soft. It's no big deal. That's not really what made me so mad."

"No, I know, but still."

"Yeah, thanks, but the point is, I got angry and I kicked a hole in the wall and my mom ran in and I told her what was happening. We got in the car and drove to my dad's office, and she started shouting at him in front of other people, and then, well . . ."

"What?" I asked.

"I don't really remember, honestly. Sometimes, when I get really stressed, I just kind of lose myself? Like I go into some trance, my ears start ringing. I feel kind of fuzzy and hot. And I can kind of be . . . destructive, I guess. Not often, right? But sometimes. Anyways, my mom says that I jumped on my dad and tried to claw his eyes out and some of my dad's employees had to drag me off of him and hold me down. Like, they sat on me for a pretty long time. They said I was speaking in tongues or something."

"Jesus, Zeke," I said, but I kind of wished that I had been able to do that to my dad.

"My dad's secretary asked if she should call the cops, and he said not to. He said we'd get me into a hospital or something, but my mom nixed that. She packed us up, and we drove here because this is where my grandmother lives. I guess my mom grew up here, but she never really talked about it, and she doesn't seem so jazzed about being back. So we're here until my mom decides what to do about my dad. She says we might be here forever or we might go back in a month. She just doesn't know."

"That sucks," I told him.

"And, I don't know, I want to go back home. I miss my house, you know? I have to go back to school at the end of the summer, right? But I don't really feel like it would be so great if my mom just went back to him. Unless he really changed. But how long would it take for someone like that to change? It feels like it could be a long time."

"My dad left us," I told him. "Two years ago. He got his secretary pregnant, and he told my mom just a few days before their anniversary because the secretary was getting mad at him for not telling my mom, and then a few days later, he and this woman moved up north. I guess he'd been planning it for a while. He got a transfer. I think it was a promotion. I don't know. He kept saying 'a fresh start,' but he meant for him and this woman and, you know, that dumb baby. It's a girl. And you know what they named it?"

"What?" he asked.

"Frances," I said. "That's my grandmother's name, his mom. I never even knew her; she died when I was little. But still. I mean, that's my name."

"That's fucked up," he admitted.

"I thought so," I said. "My mom really thought so."

"Does he call the baby Frankie?" he asked.

"I'm afraid to ask," I said. "He sent us a birth announcement, and it was all fancy so it just said *Frances*."

"Do you talk to him?" he asked.

"Never," I said. "He sends us money because he has to, but I don't talk to him. I'll never talk to him."

"I haven't talked to my dad since we moved here," Zeke told me. "I keep thinking maybe he'll call, but he doesn't. Maybe he doesn't have our number."

"Would you talk to him if he called?" I asked. I felt like his answer was important.

"Probably not. Not because I don't want to talk to him, but I feel like it would hurt his feelings if I shut him out. Like, he should be punished, right?"

"He should be," I told him. I wanted to grab his hand for emphasis, but I was weird around boys. I was weird around people in general. I didn't like touching people or being touched. But Zeke needed to know. You had to choose sides. And you always chose the person who didn't fuck everything up. You chose the person who was stuck with you.

"So," he said, looking up at me. "We're both kind of alone in the same way, right?"

"I guess so," I said. He looked like he might kiss me. Or maybe not. I'd never been this close to a boy. I knew there had to be a moment, some signal, that regular people could sense in order to go from being people who didn't kiss to being people who kissed. What the hell was it? How could I make sure not to do it until the exact right moment? His eyes were so dark, but they kind of twinkled. I felt light-headed.

"Are you hungry?" I asked him, jumping up from the sofa. "Do you want something to eat?"

"Um, sure," he said. "I'm hungry." And before he could even finish talking, I was running into the kitchen, opening the fridge, feeling the cool air on my face. Was this how love worked? You shared something personal, stood close to each other? I wasn't attracted to him. I didn't know him. All I knew was that we both had dads who sucked. All I knew was that we were both alone.

Zeke was standing at the kitchen counter. I turned to face him, shutting the door to the fridge. There wasn't much in there. I didn't know what to do. The house felt really empty. So I just said something to break up the silence.

"I'm a writer," I told him.

"Really?" he replied. He seemed impressed.

"Well, I mean, I want to be. That's what I want to do. I want to write books."

"That's cool," he said. "I like books. Stephen King? You like him?"

"He's okay," I said, but I actually didn't like him all that much. I liked southern writers, because that's what my mom taught me to love. I liked badass women southern writers like Flannery O'Connor and Carson McCullers. I liked Dorothy Allison and Bobbie Ann Mason and Alice Walker.

Oh, but really, truly, I loved Carolyn Keene. I loved Nancy Drew books. I loved the Dana Girls. And maybe I was too old for those books now, but I still read them, over and over. I didn't want to get into all of that with Zeke. If he had never read *The Member of the Wedding*, then I might cry. It would make me so sad.

"I like Philip K. Dick," he said, and I had no idea who that was. We were getting nowhere.

"I'm writing a book," I said. I'd never told anyone. Not even my mom, who would have been delighted to hear it. "It's like Nancy Drew, you know? But, she's bad. She's the one doing the crimes. And her dad is the police chief, but she keeps outsmarting him. And her sister is the girl detective, but she's not very good at it."

"Is it for kids?" Zeke asked, confused.

"I honestly don't know," I admitted. "I haven't figured it all out yet."

"Well . . . cool," Zeke said, and I believed him. "I want to be an artist," he told me, like we were both admitting that we weren't human. We didn't understand how normal this was, to be young, to believe that you were destined to make beautiful things.

"What kind of artist?" I asked him.

"Comic books," he told me. "Drawings? Weird stuff, really." His eyes lit up. He looked so happy. "And real art, too. Like, big things, complicated things. I want to make something that everyone in the world will see. And they'll remember it. And they won't totally understand it."

"I know what you mean," and I did.

"That's what we should do this summer," he said, like a lightbulb appeared over his head. He, honest to god, snapped his fingers.

"What?" I asked him.

"We should make stuff," he said.

"Well," I said, nervous, "I'm still working on the novel. It's not finished. It's just a rough draft, really."

"Okay, okay," he said. "We can figure it out. It would be fun to do something together, though."

"Just spend all summer making art?" I asked, confused.

"All summer," he said. "What else were you gonna do?"

"Okay," I told him, nodding. "But what if your dad fixes himself and you go back in a few weeks?"

He thought about this. "I don't think that's gonna happen," he told me, and we both laughed.

And that was it. That was going to be our summer. If something happened to me, it would happen to him. The next few months opened up, turned shimmery in the heat. We'd make something.

So, we were friends now. And maybe, by August, we'd be best friends. It had been a long time since I'd had a best friend. Zeke was still smiling, still staring at me, like I was supposed to say something, like I was supposed to do something important. I felt like if I did the wrong thing right now, if I messed up, it would all go wrong. But I was frozen, staring at him. Finally, he said, "So are we gonna eat lunch?"

I took such a deep breath. "Oh, yeah, sure. Let's, um, let's go to Hardee's," I told him. "My brother works there. He'll give us free fries."

And after I scrounged around my room for money, we went outside, where my shitty Honda Civic was parked in the driveway. I tried to remember what was in the cassette player, if it was cool. Maybe it wouldn't matter to Zeke. Right now, with the sun so high in the sky, we walked side by side. We'd make art later. There was, I thought, so much time.

Three

ONLY TWO DAYS LATER, WE WERE COMPLETELY BORED OUT OF our minds. It's weird, but things I did on my own and had no problems with, like dumping out my drawer of rolled-up socks and then trying to knock down an old My Little Pony on my dresser, felt sad and childish when another person saw me do them.

"What did you do for fun before I started coming over?" Zeke asked me, genuinely curious.

"This!" I said, holding up a sock ball, hitting Rosedust so hard that the toy skittered across the dresser and fell onto the floor.

"Maybe," he said gently, like trying to talk someone off the edge of a cliff, "we could think of something else to do." Everything he said, no matter how innocuous, sounded like he wanted to make out with me. I felt like maybe my anxiety around people was because I'd never kissed anyone before, and that if I just did it, I'd calm down a little, stop being so strange. But I was just too much of a prude, I guess.

I'd had friends, boys and girls, in elementary school and junior high, but it seemed like they subsequently matured in ways that my own body and brain refused to allow. They started liking sports. They started drinking and going to parties, smoking weed. They started having sex, or at least doing stuff that made me blush when I overheard them talking about it. There would be a Nancy Drew book, which I'd read four times already, hidden in my backpack, and I'd nod along while a girl I'd known since I was four years old talked about this boy I'd known since I was six trying to put his finger *inside* of her. No, thank you.

At the heart of it, I'd been normal, I think, with sleepovers and friends, and then slowly they'd drifted away. I'd talk to them sometimes in class, or I'd sit with people at lunch, but would realize they were talking about things they'd done over the weekend that I had no idea about. And I'd pretend that it didn't matter, because, honestly, I didn't want to go to the mall and look at clothes. I didn't want to watch the boys play basketball and cheer them on. I wanted other things, but I didn't know how to ask for them. By the time I realized I was kind of alone, that I didn't have any real friends, my dad ended up leaving us, and I was so angry and sad and there was no one to tell. And, you know, when your dad marries his secretary and leaves your mom all alone with four kids and not much money, people get a little weird around you. So I kept it inside of me, and that weirdness and sadness vibrated all the time, and maybe I'd just been waiting for someone who wanted me.

Zeke was staring at me, smiling, no pressure, just trying to find ways to pass the time, and I finally got inspiration. I finally had something decent for him. And I laughed, this barking sound, and said, "Well, I have an idea. I don't know if it'll work, though. I don't know if you'd even like it."

"Is it drugs?" Zeke asked, wary. "I don't want to do that." Goddamn, we were both so twitchy, so afraid.

"What? No," I said, happy that I wasn't the only one who was a square. "Just come on."

I led him to our huge garage, which had become kind of scary in its disarray, boxes of junk stacked to the ceiling, stuff my dad hadn't bothered to take with him and my mom hadn't thrown out. After he left us, she refused to even come out here. I showed Zeke how to navigate around the junk to a corner of the room. "This is kind of cool," I said, having forgotten about its existence until this very afternoon. Hidden under a tarp and obscured by water skis and a ladder, there was an old Xerox copier.

"It's broken right now," I said, "but I thought you might want to look at it."

"You have a photocopy machine?" he asked, confused.

"Yeah," I said.

"Why?" he asked.

"My brothers stole it last year," I told him.

It was true. One morning, I woke up in my bed and was surrounded by fifty or sixty photocopies of my brothers' butts, all taped to the walls in my room. It took me a few seconds to figure out what they were, these strange white moons, and then I screamed. The triplets ran into the room, laughing. My mom yelled up to see what was going on, but seemed to give up when none of us replied.

They told me how, the night before, they'd gone to the high school and pried open the lock to one of the storage buildings out back, packed to overflowing with old equipment. They'd seen the copier, plus dozens of boxes of toner, and even some stacks of paper, and thought it might be worth something. So they loaded it into the van they all shared and brought it home. And, drunk, they decided they'd make copies of their asses. "Things got out of hand," Andrew admitted. "There's like, three hundred copies of our butts." I told them to get out of my room, and then I spent the next five minutes ripping down the photocopies, wadding them into balls, and stuffing them into my wastepaper basket. But there were too many of them, and they spilled out onto the floor, slowly opening like flowers, my brothers' bright white asses.

The copier was an old model from the late eighties, and nobody that my brothers knew wanted to buy it, and then they broke it after sitting on it a hundred times and they spent a whole day arguing about which one of them had ruined it. It was this huge piece of junk now, and my mom had told them a hundred times to get rid of it, and they told her that they would, but they just covered it with a tarp and forgot about it. That was how it worked. If you couldn't see it, if you pushed it into a dark corner, it didn't exist. But here it was. I was claiming it. It was mine now. Ours.

"This could be pretty cool," Zeke admitted.

"Well, maybe, but my dumbass brothers broke it. We could try to fix it, but maybe we could just go to the library and use that one."

"Broke it how?"

"They broke it so it doesn't work anymore," I said, though it didn't really seem to register with Zeke.

He looked at the machine, opening the lid, and then rubbed his chin. "Did they read the manual?" he asked.

"Did my brothers read the manual? Are you serious?"

"Did they?"

"No!" I shouted. "They broke it with their asses and that was that."

We found an extension cord and turned it on, the light blinking, but nothing happened when he pushed the button to copy. I just watched him as he went through a little checklist of possible issues, each time whispering, "No, okay, no," and moving on, opening up the machine, poking around.

Just as I was about to suggest that we quit, Zeke said, "Oh, wait!" I watched him wriggle his fingers inside the copier, and then he gently, little by little, pulled out a crumpled piece of paper, folded like an accordion, as if the copier had done origami, and then he handed the sheet to me. I smoothed it out. It was the ass of one of my stupid brothers.

"It was just jammed in there," he said, smiling.

Now Zeke placed his palm down on the glass and made a copy, which took a while, and then there was his hand, all the lines running across his palm. It worked. I knew this didn't make Zeke a genius, but it did make him smarter than my brothers, the only boys I spent time around, so I felt like I'd made a good choice for the summer.

"If I moved my hand all over the glass," he said, "it would be like an animation. Like a cartoon."

"But we'd need some kind of machine to flip the pages," I said. "Or a stop-motion camera, right?"

"I guess," he said, a little disappointed.

Still, we spent the next hour wandering around the garage, picking out items to place on the glass of the copier. We liked how, if the object was too big, it distorted the image, made it seem unreal. Then I found an old *Vogue* magazine and tore out a photo of Cher, her long black hair and smoky eyeliner. I pushed the button, but then started to drag the photo across the glass. The copy that the machine spat out showed half of Cher's face as it regularly appeared, but then the rest of the image smeared across the page, streaking, like she was melting sideways.

"Oh, that's cool!" Zeke said, impressed. He ripped out a page that featured some random model, and then made a kind of zigzag with the image as the light emanated from the machine. It wasn't super clear, but the result was trippy, slightly ominous.

"Can you make art with a copy machine?" I asked him.

He smiled. "Maybe," he replied. "Why not?"

We were teenagers in the middle of nowhere in Tennessee. We didn't know about Xerox art or Andy Warhol or anything like that. We thought we'd made it up. And I guess, for us, we had.

I pressed one side of my face against the glass, and the result made me look like some baby in the womb, my features all flattened out.

"Wait," Zeke said. "If we put our faces side by side, it'll be like those optical illusions where you see either two faces in profile or a vase. Yeah?"

"Oh," I said, "okay, yeah."

So we put our faces against the glass, our mouths so close together. "Wait," Zeke said, seemingly unfazed by the proximity of our lips, "I'm trying to find the button."

What resulted didn't really look like an optical illusion. It looked like two dead people, two kids who had suddenly been pulled into a black hole or something.

"It's cool, though," Zeke said. "It looks like an album cover for a death metal band."

"Let's try again," I said. I felt resolute. I felt like we were making something important. I felt like, I don't know, I was in control. I was making the decisions. And as long as I was choosing, it was okay.

So we put our faces next to each other, but this time, when he pushed the button, I inched forward and kissed him, our mouths touching, this light slowly streaming past us. It didn't feel real at all, which is what I thought kissing would be like. And we had to hold it, until the copier finished humming. My first kiss.

"Um," Zeke said, bumping his head on the copier. "What did you do that for?"

"I don't know," I said, which was true. "I've never kissed anyone before."

"Me either," he told me.

"And this felt like a nice way to do it," I said. "Like, you know, art."

We looked at the copy that the machine spat out. We looked so ugly, our faces smashed together, but the blackness around us made it seem like a fairy tale. Was this what people looked like when they kissed? I guessed it wasn't. It was what people looked like when they kissed against the glass of a copier. It's what, I imagined, art looked like. Ugly and beautiful at the same time.

"I'm sorry I didn't ask first," I said, now very embarrassed. "I just, I don't know, wanted to finally do it. So it wouldn't be so scary. So I could move on and be normal."

Zeke didn't say anything. I thought he might kiss me for real, not for art but for real. But he didn't. He smiled, sheepish, like he couldn't control his mouth, and then said, "This could be fun."

I thought he was talking about kissing but realized he was looking at the copier. "We could do something weird with this," he went on.

"Weird," I said, like it was a magic word, like all I had to do was say it out loud and my world would change.

Four

I DON'T THINK EITHER ONE OF US UNDERSTOOD HOW HARD IT was to create something good. We were smart kids, made excellent grades. Our teachers thought we were gifted because we could read and write at a slightly elevated level, because if we were gifted, then they weren't wasting their lives teaching burnouts. Well, Zeke really was gifted, I think. He went to some fancy private school in Memphis, where they wore uniforms, where there was an actual class on sequential art and you could take it for actual credit. But that summer, away from school and classes and teachers, we were on our own, unsupervised, and we realized that we didn't know what we were doing.

So for the next week, we sat at the table in my kitchen, drinking flavored instant coffee, and he drew his comics and I wrote my weird girl detective novel in my notebook, and occasionally we would brush our legs against each other, the slightest friction making my armpits sweat like crazy. We were sixteen. How did you prevent your life from turning into something so boring that no one wanted to know about it? How did you make yourself special?

We made collages from my mom's old issues of *Glamour*, cutting out the mouths of every model, their pearly white teeth and plump lips. I couldn't figure out what was creepier, the pile of mouths or all the discarded pictures of these beautiful women, jagged holes where their mouths had once been. We cut out the word *beauty* every time we saw it, until we'd covered a whole page with the word, until it looked like a different language, unrecognizable to us. We took all the sample strips of perfume, twenty or thirty of them with names like Fahrenheit 180 and Ransom, and rubbed them on our wrists until the combined smell became so overwhelming that we got sick. But I'd hold my arm out and Zeke would take it like it was a precious artifact from a museum. And he'd sniff and sniff, and I'd pray that he couldn't smell me, what was underneath all that perfume, because I knew it would smell so desperate, so lonely.

And we'd kiss. It was the strangest kind of kissing, where our lips would touch and then lock onto each other for ten minutes at a time, but the rest of our bodies barely even touched. It would have been so much easier to just have sex, to get it over with, but I was terrified of getting pregnant, of getting some disease. I was terrified of what my body might do under those circumstances, what his would do. So we stayed fully clothed, hands at our sides, sucking on our faces until our mouths were red and angry. He tasted like celery, like rabbit food, every single time, and I loved it. I was afraid to ask him what I tasted like.

And then, one time, while we were sitting on the couch in the living room, making out, my mom unlocked the front door and walked into the house. "Whoa," she said when she saw us, an actual sucking sound made when we pulled apart, scrambling to opposite sides of the couch. She smiled, trying not to laugh. Zeke had taken out his Velcro wallet and was inspecting his library card, like it was very important to make sure that he still had it. I just sat there, looking down at my feet, my lips tingling.

"Well . . . hello," my mom said. "Who is this young man?"

"This is Zeke," I finally said, my face burning red with embarrassment. "He's new in town."

"Okay, okay, okay," my mom said, nodding. "Hey, Zeke."

"Hello, Mrs. . . . um . . . Hey there," he said. "I don't know Frankie's last name."

"Well, her last name is different from mine anyways," she said. "You can call me Carrie, though."

"Hello, Carrie," he said. He was still holding that library card, like maybe my mom was going to ask for it.

"We've been hanging out," I said. "Zeke is an artist."

"Okay, cool," my mom said, still nodding, trying to figure out what in the world I was doing with a boy in the house, because I had never even been on a date, had not, to her knowledge, spoken to a boy in years.

"I draw," Zeke said.

"So you guys have just made this little artist colony here in the house while everybody else is away?" she asked.

"Kind of?" I said.

"Well, it's nice to meet you, Zeke. Frankie has not told me a thing about you, but you are welcome to come over anytime. In fact, would you like to have dinner with us tonight? I'd love to hear your story."

"Well, I don't know," Zeke replied, looking over at me. "I mean, I guess I could ask my mom if it's okay."

"Sure thing," my mom said. "If she wants to talk to me, I'm happy to vouch for Frankie. I mean, I'm sure you told your mom about this cool new friend that you've met. I'm sure you'd tell your mom something important like that."

"Mom, it's just—" I started, but just gave up. I knew she wasn't really upset. She wasn't that kind of mom.

"My mom is . . . she's kind of preoccupied right now," Zeke said. "I don't think she'll mind."

"Then it's settled," my mom said. "I just came home to pick up something, and then I have to get back to work. I guess . . . I guess I'll see you when I come back."

"Nice to meet you," Zeke said. He finally put the library card back in his wallet and Velcroed it shut.

And then she was gone. And it was just me and Zeke.

"Maybe we should make art," he said, just like that, like art was cookies or microwave popcorn. Like if anything was going to keep us from having sex, from doing something we'd regret, it would be art.

"Okay," I said, still flushed, still tasting celery, "let's make art."

We knelt on the floor in my musty garage, baking, making copies of anything that seemed interesting. I'd found a photo of my mom and dad and I used scissors to make a jagged separation between them, cutting the photo in half. I pasted them to the edges of a piece of copy paper, and then Zeke drew all these little designs in the gap between them, snakes wrapped around knives, lightning bolts, a fist punching out of a grave. Then we put it on the copy machine and looked at the black-and-white image it spat out. It made me sad. I wondered if that was kind of the purpose of art, maybe, to make you see things that you knew but couldn't say out loud.

"This isn't bad," Zeke said. "This is pretty cool."

"I kind of want to throw it away," I said. "I think I'd feel awful if my mom ever saw this."

"I think maybe art is supposed to make your family uncomfortable," he offered.

"Well, I guess I'm not quite an artist yet," I said, "because I don't want her to see it." I crumpled up the original and the copy and tossed them into the garbage can.

We sat on the cement floor, not sure what to do. I wanted to make out again, but I felt weird asking. Zeke was thinking about something, and so I waited to hear what he'd figured out.

"The problem," he said, "is that this is all so private. We're just making this stuff and because we're sitting in your garage, it doesn't feel like art. It's like something you'd put in your journal and no one would ever see it except you."

"Well, there's no museum or art gallery in town," I said. "So we couldn't show it off even if we wanted to."

"That's not true," he said. "In Memphis, there are graffiti artists and they just make any space into a gallery. They, like, climb up onto a building and put up a tag and then disappear before anyone sees them. And it's pretty cool. Sometimes a tag stays up for a long time, if the city can't be bothered to paint over it or blast it off."

"I don't know how to do graffiti," I said.

"Well, I don't either, but we can do something like that, right? We've got the copier, right? We can make the tag beforehand and then post it up later. It'll be faster, and it will be harder for anyone to catch us."

"Why would anyone want to catch us?" I asked. "Is it illegal to put up posters?"

"I don't know. Maybe it's a legal gray area. I mean, it's not permanent, so maybe not. But, honestly, it would be better if it was a secret."

"So . . . wait . . . now you don't want anyone to know that we made the art?"

"I guess not. It's just you and me. No one else will ever know. We'll put up all this art, maybe hide it all over town, and people will be like, *Who made this cool shit*, and we'll be like, *Wow, damn, I don't know. Someone pretty cool, I bet*, and we'll walk away and kind of whistle and keep our hands in our pockets."

"Well," I finally said, trying to understand. "I guess so."

"So now we need a tag," he said.

"What should it be?" I asked.

"Something messed up. Something really weird. Like, a mystery or a riddle that no one can solve. And it'll drive the whole town crazy."

"How do we do that?" I asked.

"You're a writer, right?" he said, smiling, getting jittery, excited. "You write something really strange, and then I'll illustrate around it. And we'll make, like, twenty copies. And hang them up in town."

"What do I write?" I asked, still not getting it.

"Anything!" he said. "Something really weird. Like, it doesn't mean anything but it also, like, kind of means something."

"That sounds hard," I admitted.

"No," he said, and now he was really amped up. His eyes were twinkling like some kind of cartoon, so black that light was sparkling off his pupils. "Don't even think about it. Just write something."

"I can't do that," I said. I felt like I couldn't match his enthusiasm and I was a failure because of it. "I can't just write something."

"Yes, you can," he said. "You're an amazing writer. Just—here—" He grabbed a piece of paper and put it in front of me. "Just write whatever comes to you."

"About what?" I asked, almost crying now.

"About Coalfield. About this town. About your life. About your stupid fucking dad. About whatever you want."

I picked up a pencil and took a deep breath, like I was trying to suck up every word in the English language. And I started tapping the paper, making these tiny little dots. Tap-tap-tap-tap and I just kept tapping. And I tried. I thought about the sun, how bright it was outside, how hot the world was getting, how pretty soon the world would overheat and we'd all die. But that wasn't what I wanted to say. I thought about my half sister, Frances, and how I could take all my baby teeth, which I'd kept in a plastic baggie, and drive to my dad's house and give them to her, like a gift. I thought about Zeke's weird, crooked little mouth. I thought about the book I was writing, the girl criminal mastermind. Her name was Evie Fastabend. She was always calling her hideout, this little abandoned shack in the woods, *the edge.* It was her code name for when she wanted to do crimes. *I need to go to the edge,* she'd announce, and then she'd ride her bike to the woods, to this rickety shed, where she had a gun wrapped up in an old T-shirt. *The edge,* I thought. *The edge. The edge. The edge. The edge.*

And then I wrote. *The edge is a shantytown*—and I took another deep breath, realized I hadn't been breathing that whole time. My vision got all fuzzy. Zeke touched my shoulder. "Are you okay?" he asked, but I was already writing more—*filled with gold seekers.*

Zeke looked over my shoulder at the paper. "That's . . . okay, that's kind of cool," he said. "I like that."

The edge is a shantytown filled with gold seekers. We are fugitives, I wrote. There was this little voice in my head, and it was telling me what to write down. And I knew that this little voice, this tiny, insistent voice, was not God and it wasn't some muse and it wasn't anyone in the world except for me. This voice was my voice. This voice was my voice and no one else's voice, and I could hear it so clearly. And it wasn't finished.

The edge is a shantytown filled with gold seekers. We are fugitives, and the law is skinny with hunger for us.

And then the voice was gone. It went way, way back inside me. And I didn't know if it would ever come back. And I finally read what was on the paper. "We are fugitives," I said to Zeke, smiling. I was starting to laugh, a little hiccup of a laugh. "We are fugitives?" I asked him.

"And the law is skinny with hunger for us," he said, smiling. It didn't make a bit of sense. It meant nothing. But Zeke understood. That was all that mattered to me.

It was the greatest thing that I'd ever written. I knew it right then. And I'd never write anything that good again. It sounded so perfect to my ears.

Zeke and I crouched down on the hard floor of the garage, said the phrase again, and then again, and then again, until it became a code. It became a code for everything that we'd ever want. It became a code that, if we met up again in fifty years, we could say this exact phrase, and we'd know. We'd know who we were.

"Can I kiss you?" Zeke asked, and I wished that he had not asked. But I also liked that he'd asked, had not taken advantage of me in that moment.

"You can kiss me," I said, and so we kissed, and I felt the tiniest little tip of his tongue touch my teeth and it made me shiver. And the whole time we kissed, I kept thinking *Wearefugitiveswearefugitiveswearefugitives*, and I knew that the law, whatever the fuck that was, was skinny with hunger for us.

Five

MY MOM WOULD BE HOME AT FIVE. THE TRIPLETS, NO IDEA, though I could count on them to be as scarce as possible while they huffed glue or had sex with girls in abandoned factories. It felt like a bomb was set to go off, and we had to defuse it without a manual. Or maybe we were building a bomb. Who knows. It felt like something was at stake, that's what I'm trying to say. I wanted to keep kissing Zeke, but the thrill of making something was competing. We had the words. Our code. The edge. Fugitives. The law. But we had to make it look nice.

Zeke had all these cool, expensive art pens and pencils, Pentel and Micron and some kind of Japanese brush pen, but I grabbed a black Crayola marker and got to work. It was a lot of words to fit on a piece of paper, so I had to make the letters small enough to leave space for Zeke's artwork, but I wanted the writing to be bold enough that you could clearly read it.

Over my shoulder, Zeke whispered the next letter, *F . . . u . . . g . . . i*, and I liked the feel of his breath on my neck, but I kept my hand steady.

When I was done, Zeke snatched the paper away before I could even reread the phrase, and he got to work with all those pens. He had something finished in his head, I knew, because his hand moved so deliberately, even though he couldn't keep the tremors of excitement from threatening to mess it up. He started by drawing these power lines, stretching across the page like tiny scars, and once he had a sense of scale, he drew these beautiful little shacks, a whole row of them, the roofs falling in. He drew bits of detritus, an old, burned-out car, a pack of wild dogs. And then, out in the open air, he drew four beds, their headboards like Gothic cathedrals, multiple children twisted up in the sheets. Finally, he pushed away from the paper, almost like he'd unplugged himself from the image, and just stared at it. So I stared, too, at the way the drawings touched up against my words, the way our two brains became this one thing. And then, careful to work around the words I'd written, he leaned over the paper and drew two giant, disembodied hands, the fingers withered and jagged, almost glowing, the way he made the shape of them echo across the page. It looked like the hands were reaching for the children in the beds, but they were suspended, never quite able to touch them.

"There," he finally said. "That's it."

"It's done?" I asked, not quite sure of myself, of us.

"I don't know," he admitted. "But maybe."

"We made it," I said, like I couldn't quite believe it, even though it was just this little piece of paper.

"But nobody will know," he reminded me. "Just you and me."

"Okay," I agreed.

"But we have to do something to make it ours," he said. He reached into his zippered bag of art supplies and got an X-Acto blade, which made me stiffen a little, shift my body away from his, hovering over the blade.

"Blood," he said, because of course he did. What else did we have, two stupid teenagers, but the blood inside of us?

"Blood?" I replied. Like I said, I wasn't big on being touched, especially not by sharp objects.

"On the page," he said. "It's symbolic, right? Is it a metaphor? Wait, what's a metaphor?"

"Not blood," I answered, though what did I know?

"It feels right," he admitted, rolling the blade between his fingers.

"Okay, then," I said, deciding to trust him. And Zeke pressed the blade against the tip of his finger, and I stared at the way the skin resisted it. I felt dizzy. Finally, the blade pushed through the skin, and he made this little gasp, and then there was nothing. Just a second or two or nothing, and then, like it was being conjured, like a magic trick, this little bubble of blood rose to the surface. He set the blade down and squeezed his finger until the blood started to drip down his finger.

"Now you," he said. I hesitated. "It doesn't hurt," he told me, and I believed him.

I took the blade, held it up to my left middle finger, and pressed the blade into the skin. But my hand slipped a little, or maybe I got scared at the last second, because I dragged the blade down the length of my finger, opening it up, and blood came so fast that I felt like I was going to pass out.

"Oh, shit!" Zeke cried out, and I said, "I think I fucked it up," but he grabbed the edge of his shirt and wrapped it around my finger, forgetting about his own wound. There wasn't a lot of blood, not as much as it seemed at first, but it was enough that we got scared. We were still kids, afraid of getting into trouble. I was bleeding, but I didn't know what to do next.

"On the paper," he said, "like, drip it on the paper?" I could tell he didn't know what he was doing, but I took my hand away from his grip and I shook my hand over the paper, like I was trying to dry it in the open air, and the blood went in all directions, little flecks of it on my face. Zeke really had to squeeze his finger to get anything, but eventually he got some on the paper, too. When it felt like I'd done enough, I put my finger in my mouth, that taste of iron on my tongue, and then I wrapped it up inside my shirt.

The blood, flecks and flecks of it, looked like stars in the sky, strange constellations, symbols and meanings. It looked beautiful, like we'd made a universe.

"We have to let it dry," he said, like all of this was perfectly normal, "and then we can make copies."

So we just sat there on the floor of the dusty, cramped garage, surrounded by things nobody wanted. I needed to get a bandage for my finger, but I didn't want to move. And Zeke asked if he could kiss me again.

"My mouth tastes like blood," I admitted.

"It's okay," he told me. So I let him kiss me. And even then, in that very moment, I knew that this was important. I knew that I would trace my whole life back to this moment, my finger bleeding, this boy's beautiful and messed-up mouth on mine, a work of art between us. I knew it would probably fuck me up. And that was fine.

Once our mouths started hurting, we went back inside the house and got some bandages from the bathroom to fix me up as best we could. It probably needed stitches, but the cut was so exact that it felt like, with a little pressure, the skin would re-form, like nothing had happened. Zeke didn't need anything, his blood already dried up, but he still put a little bandage on his finger. I wondered if this was a sign that, whatever happened this summer, I'd be the one with a scar.

Then we went back into the garage and placed our work of art on the copy machine. We closed the lid and then, hesitating for a second, we both pushed the button at the same time. The machine whirred, rumbled, and I thought that maybe all that would come out would be this curling black smoke, but no, it was just our picture, copied. Now we had two. It was already a little less special now, but maybe I was looking at it the wrong way. Maybe it doubled in power. Something had happened, that was all that mattered. We observed the copy, not quite the original, everything just a little blurry at the edges, a little more dreamlike. Nothing could be as perfect as the one we had made together, just the two of us. But it was okay. We just needed more of them.

"Ten copies?" Zeke said, and the machine hummed, time passed, and there were ten more copies.

"Maybe, like, ten more?" I offered, and Zeke nodded.

Ten more, and we felt the weight of the copies. It didn't seem like enough.

"Fifty more?" he asked.

"A hundred, I think," I replied.

"Yeah, okay," he said.

"We can always make more, I guess," I said, because, really, truly, I wanted a million of them now.

So we made a hundred more. We now had one hundred and twenty copies of this weird thing. It felt like alchemy, like all those brooms in *Fantasia*, like the world was finally big enough for the things that we cared about, that we'd make it ourselves.

When we were done making copies, we covered up the Xerox machine again, put the junk on top of it so no one would know what we'd been doing. We gathered up our stuff and went back into the house. Zeke counted out sixty for him and sixty for me, and we put them inside our backpacks. Pretty soon my mom would be home, my brothers. And they would have no idea what we'd done. They'd think that maybe we had sex, those idiots, those dumbos. They wouldn't know what we'd brought into this world.

"What about the original?" I asked, holding it up.

"You keep it," he said, maybe the sweetest thing anyone had ever done for me in my life. I had hoped for this, did not want it to be out of my possession.

"Yeah," he went on. "You have the copier, right? So you keep the original. But be careful. Don't lose it. Don't let anyone find it. Ever. For the rest of your life, you have to keep it, okay?"

"I will," I said, as serious as I'd ever been about anything.

"The edge is a shantytown filled with gold seekers," he told me.

"We are fugitives," I said, smiling, "and the law is skinny with hunger for us."

And then we just stood in my living room, not sure what to do next. In our heads, we were both saying the words, over and over, until we had them memorized. We sat there, the words rolling on a loop, again and again, until they didn't mean anything, again and again, until they meant something, again and again, until they meant everything.

Okay, yes, we were going insane, maybe. We'd kissed and our prudish brains couldn't handle it, so we invented some mantra that would unlock the mysteries of the universe. We'd created meaning where there was none, but, I don't know, isn't that art? Or at least I think it's the kind of art that I like, where the obsession of one person envelops other people, transforms them. But I didn't have any theories then. I just had those words, those little kids in their beds and those giant hands reaching out for them. Meaning would have to come later.

MY MOM SHOWED UP WITH FOUR LARGE PIZZAS FROM TWINS, A rare treat, and I could see that she was trying to impress Zeke. I didn't want to tell her that Zeke was from Memphis, a real city, and pizza wouldn't impress him. But, honestly, Zeke looked pretty goddamned psyched to eat pizza.

"How's the art coming along?" she asked as she breezed into the kitchen.

"Great!" we both shouted, way too loud. I'm sure my mom thought we'd been tentatively exploring each other's bodies, which made me want to gag, but she just nodded. It was a weird thing. Before the divorce, my mom had been kind of strict, the triplets constantly wrecking shit as she sternly tried to wrangle them. She had no patience for people who might complicate her life or create more work for her, was always rolling her eyes at how stupid everyone else was. She made checklists that no one else ever checked. She frowned a lot. I was slightly afraid of her, even though I knew that she loved me. And though I knew the divorce had messed her up, it had also seemed to relax her, like the bad thing had finally happened and she didn't have to keep waiting for it. She chilled out. The triplets, if they burned down the Dairy Queen, well, that was someone else's problem. If I invited some strange boy into our house and made out with him, who was she to intervene? We were eating pizza on a weekday. She was the coolest mom in Coalfield.

One by one, like a Xerox had spit them out, the triplets trudged into the house, each of them reeking of weed and french fry grease. We told them that we had pizza, and they just grunted and disappeared into the room they all shared. The smell in that room, the air. I cannot describe it.

Mom put the pizzas in the oven to keep them warm and Zeke and I started setting the table. "What happened to your hand?" she asked me.

"What now?" I asked, dropping a fork onto the table, so much noise.

"And *your* hand?" she asked Zeke, pointing at his tiny, laughable wound.

"Hmm," Zeke said, like she'd asked him a philosophical question.

"Did you guys do a blood oath or something?" my mom asked, like she'd heard about this from Phil Donahue.

"No!" I said, too loud. "God, Mom, we didn't do any kind of blood oath."

"It's unsanitary," my mom offered very gently.

"I sliced my finger cutting up some apples for a healthy snack," I finally told her. Zeke nodded, though he looked a little pained, like he wished he'd thought of that.

"And this," Zeke said, holding up his finger for my mom to inspect, "was, like, a previous accident. I came here today wearing this Band-Aid."

"Oh," my mom said, "okay, then." She was smiling like, what did it really matter? She'd already seen us making out. She knew something was going on. "Boys!" she shouted to my brothers, which made Zeke flinch. And they rambled into the room. I don't think they had realized that Zeke was in the house yet. It wasn't until we were all seated, eating our pizza, and my mom asked Zeke a question that my brothers all looked up in wonder at this strange name, this strange boy in our house. Then they went back to wolfing down pizza.

"So," my mom asked Zeke. "What brings you to Coalfield?"

"Well," Zeke began, looking at me as if we'd rehearsed an answer earlier today, "we're here just, like, visiting my grandmother. My mom grew up in Coalfield."

"Oh, really?" my mom replied, getting somewhere. "What's her name?"

"Cydney," Zeke replied. "Cydney Hudson when she lived in Coalfield."

"Oh!" my mom shouted, her eyes so big. "I know Cydney! She was a few years behind me in school. She was, what's the word, like some kind of kid genius."

"A prodigy?" Zeke offered.

"Exactly. A musical prodigy."

"That's right," Zeke said. "Or, I mean, that's what my mom tells me." He turned to me and just said, "Violin."

"She got this fancy scholarship to Juilliard, I remember," my mom continued. "I haven't seen her since."

"That's her," Zeke replied.

"Is she famous?" my mom asked him, seeming a little starstruck. "I mean, in classical music circles?"

"No," Zeke said. "I don't think so."

"Oh," my mom said, looking so disappointed. "It was such a big deal when she got that scholarship. I remember the paper wrote a big article about it. And she was a prodigy. I haven't thought of her a lot, but when I did, I figured she was in New York, playing concerts for, like, the prime minister of Japan or something."

"Well, no," Zeke said, taking his mother's artistic failures very well, I have to say. "My mom said everyone at Juilliard was a prodigy. She got a job at the Memphis Symphony Orchestra and then she met my dad and they got married and, I guess, I mean, you know, she had me."

"Well . . . that's great," my mom said. "Tell her that Carrie Neal says hello."

"Are you guys boyfriend and girlfriend?" Andrew interrupted, pointing the tip of his slice of pizza at Zeke in a way that only my brothers could make look threatening.

"No!" I interjected, reaching my hand out ineffectually toward Zeke, like we'd stopped short in the car and I was protecting him.

"No?" my mom asked, looking a little amused. "Is that right?"

"Well," Zeke said, looking down at his empty plate, "I mean, it's complicated, right?"

I wanted him to shut up, not to give my brothers anything that they could use against me, but he kept going. "I'm just here for the summer, so that's . . . you know, a temporary . . . kind of a nonpermanent situation."

"Nonpermanent does not sound encouraging," my mother offered.

"We're friends," I finally said. "We're *FRIENDS*."

"Good friends," Zeke offered, and I nodded to him like, *Yeah, duh*, but also like, *Shut up, my brothers will try to ruin me.*

"Well, I for one think it's great that Frankie has found such a good friend for the summer."

"Frankie has no friends," Brian told Zeke, like maybe he was stupid and didn't understand how weird I was.

"Well," Zeke said, now reaching across the table for another slice of pizza, "I feel, like, honored, then," and I blushed so hard that the triplets all made the same satisfied expression, their job done, before they went back to destroying the rest of the pizza.

After we'd washed the dishes, I told my mom that Zeke and I were going to get some ice cream at the Dairy Queen and then I'd take Zeke home. She shook Zeke's hand and said he seemed like a fine young man, and Zeke seemed stricken but did his best to smile. Both of us reached for our backpacks, the copies of our art hidden inside them, and we were gone.

And I can't quite explain it, the weirdness of this feeling, when we stepped out of the house for the first time in many,

many hours. We were outside, in the open air, and the copies were with us. Everything felt so much bigger, more important. It was, honestly, a little hard to breathe.

"Are you ready to do this?" Zeke asked, so tenderly, a kind boy.

"I guess so," I said, though I wasn't sure if I was.

"Where should we go?" he asked me, and I was like, what? "Where should we hang these copies?" he continued. "I'm not from here, so I don't know the best place for, like, optimal exposure."

"Oh," I said. "I guess, like, maybe the square? It's got a movie theater and ice cream shop. The courthouse is in the center of it if we wanted to be, like, I don't know, political about it."

"Okay," he said, nodding. "Let's go to the square."

We got in my car, and we didn't say another word for the twelve minutes that it took to get to the town square. There were a fair number of teenagers milling around the entrance to the movie theater, and it suddenly occurred to me how embarrassing it would be for somebody I knew to see me hang up this picture.

"Maybe," I offered, "over there, where that insurance company is?" It was dark, closed for the night, a sign for a Boy Scouts raffle hanging in the window.

"Yeah," Zeke replied. "That's cool."

So we stepped out of my car, our backpacks slung over our shoulders, and we normally, so normally it doesn't even need to be mentioned, walked over to the entrance of the insurance company.

"Should we use one of yours?" Zeke asked me. He looked really nervous, kind of sweating in the heat. The sun hadn't even fully set. We were very exposed. But no one cared. We were invisible.

"Yeah, we can use one of mine," I told him, and I carefully unzipped my backpack. I pulled out a sheet of paper, but another one was stuck to it and came with it, and then I awkwardly tried to get the stray piece of paper to fit back in the backpack but it wasn't going in. Finally, I gave up, crumpled up the piece of paper, awkwardly shoved it into my pocket, and then took the clean sheet and . . . well, okay. Right at that moment I realized that we had no tape. No way to hang up our art.

"How do I hang it up?" I asked, pressing the picture against the glass like it would just stick somehow.

"Oh, shit," Zeke whispered, his eyes huge. "Oh, fuck. We gotta abort this mission, I think."

"Let's go back to the car," I said, "and figure this out."

We both kind of duck-walked very suspiciously back to my car, and I fumbled for my keys to unlock the doors, and we dove into the front seats.

"That was not good," he admitted.

"We need, like, tape. Nails. Pushpins. Staples. A staple gun," I told him.

"Where can we get that stuff?" he asked.

"At the Wal-Mart?" I offered. "They have everything, pretty much."

"Okay, let's go there," he said, visibly deflating.

"Should we just try again another time?" I asked.

"No," he said, so petulant. "We have to do it tonight."

"Okay. Then let's go get some supplies." Why, I wondered, was true art so hard to make? Why did it never turn out quite the way that you envisioned it? Why were Zeke and I doomed to live the life of an artist? But we'd fix it, I decided. We'd go to Wal-Mart. Nothing would stop us.

We instantly separated inside the store, and I bought the staple gun and staples, while Zeke went into another line and bought duct tape and pushpins, which we thought was what criminal masterminds would do. I felt a little giddy, looking over at Zeke, a few cashiers over, and we both smiled, so happy to be closer to our goal. We met up near the entrance, and I noticed the bulletin board that had missing-child posters and various official notices.

I reached into my pocket and produced the crumpled-up copy from earlier in the evening. Zeke look alarmed, instinctively reached out for the paper, but I pulled back. "Right now?" he asked, and I nodded.

I handed my shopping bag to Zeke and smoothed out the paper as best I could, the effect adding some character to the copy, like some old map or something. I took a pushpin from one of the missing-kid posters, a boy named Zachary who had been missing for two years, and tacked up our work in the corner of the bulletin board. We stood there for a second, staring at it, those hands, my words. It felt right. This was the thing about having more than a hundred copies of our poster: we didn't have to worry too much about placement. If we put up enough of them, the art would do the real work.

"It looks amazing," I said to Zeke, who nodded. He seemed pretty nervous, constantly looking around to see if anyone noticed us, even though nobody cared.

"Let's keep doing it," I said, and we got in the car, speeding back to the square, leaving a piece of ourselves behind, waiting to be discovered.

BY THE TIME I DROPPED OFF ZEKE AND RETURNED TO MY OWN home, we'd put up sixty-three posters, working as quickly as possible, undetected. We stapled them to telephone poles, taped them to the windows of businesses, folded them up and hid them in the aisles of the grocery store. We covered a brick wall behind the movie theater in the square, rows upon rows. We put a few in some random mailboxes on the way to Zeke's grandmother's house. And we still had so many. But also, in my head, we didn't have nearly enough. We needed more. We needed to put up more of them. The whole town. I wished we had an airplane that we could fly over Coalfield, dumping out copy after copy on the unsuspecting citizens below. The whole experience felt like what drugs must have felt like. It was the high of doing something weird, not knowing the outcome. I imagined my wild brothers had felt this so many times that they were numb to it. But for Zeke and me, well-behaved dorks, it was amazing. And we were together. We hadn't even made out. We were too interested in the copies. Each time we looked at each other, we were holding up another copy of our art, affixing it to the world. It felt important to us. We were important.

And when I dropped off Zeke, too afraid to come inside and meet his mom and grandmother, he kissed me softly on the cheek. "I really like you," he told me.

"I like you, too," I replied.

"We can keep doing this?" he asked, meaning, I assumed, everything. The posters, my house, the kissing, Pop-Tarts, skulking around every square inch of the town.

"All summer," I said.

"Maybe even longer," he said hopefully, which made me blush. I kissed him on the lips and then he was gone. On the drive back to my house, I left my car running at an empty four-way stop, taped one of the posters to the stop sign, and then ran back to my car, feeling so wild. I drove exactly five miles above the speed limit through residential streets. I felt like I was flying.

I WOKE UP LATER THAT NIGHT BECAUSE MY MOM WAS SHAKING me, and I startled awake. "Jesus, Mom?" I said, my voice scratchy, my head so heavy.

"I'm sorry, sweetie," she said, kind of whispering but also kind of shouting. It was a strange effect. I wasn't sure if I was dreaming. "I know it's late, but I really want to talk to you."

"Right now?" I asked.

"Yes, right now," she said. "Here, move over, jeez, just let me . . . Frankie? Wake up, okay? Just scoot over so I can sit down."

I sighed as deeply as possible, long enough that I was starting to fall back asleep, and then I slumped over a few inches so she could sit on the bed.

"Now, I know I was acting all cool and hip this afternoon, you remember? When I found you two . . . kissing, I guess you'd call it? And Zeke seems like a sweet kid. And I don't want to mess you up any more than . . . well, I just don't want to put a lot of unnecessary pressure on you, but I've been up all night. I can't sleep."

"What is it, Mom?" I asked, so grumpy, but also kind of terrified that she'd somehow found out about the art, the Xerox machine, the posters hanging up in town.

"I just . . . I know we talked about all of this a few years ago, but it didn't really feel real to me then. Now I feel like I just need to reiterate some of those talking points, okay?"

"*What is it, Mom?*" I said.

"You're a young woman, and your body is your body, and that's fine, I respect that. And it's natural, like we talked about before, to have desires."

"Gross," I said. "Desires."

"Frankie, just shut up for a second," she continued. "If you're going to be physical . . . you know, *have sex*—there, I said it. If you have sex with Zeke, I want you to use protection. You have to use protection. That's nonnegotiable."

"Mom, this is embarrassing. I'm not going to have sex with Zeke. It's fine."

"Look," my mom now said, reaching into the pocket of her bathrobe, "just take these condoms, okay. Frankie? Just take them."

"I don't want these condoms," I told her.

"You have to take them. That's nonnegotiable. And that's what you tell Zeke, too, okay? Say, *it's nonnegotiable*. Let me hear you say it."

"Where did you get them?" I asked her.

"That's not the point, sweetie," she replied.

"The box is already opened," I said, inspecting it in the dark. "Some of them are missing, I think."

"Frankie! Focus, please. Just keep them in case. I can tell you this with one hundred percent certainty. You do not want a baby at your age. Or . . . or three babies. Can you even imagine, Frankie? Three babies, all at once? You're still just a kid. You don't want that."

"Okay, okay," I finally said. I put the box under my pillow. "Thank you, Mom. Thank you for caring about me."

"I do care about you, sweetie," she said. "So much."

"I know," I said.

"I'm going to be in the kitchen, okay? I'm not going to sleep tonight, I don't think. I think I might make a cake or something for you to give to Zeke's mom? How does that sound?"

"Mom," I said. "I'm so tired."

"Good night, sweetie," she finally said. "Go back to bed."

After she left, I closed my eyes and whispered to myself, *The edge is a shantytown filled with gold seekers. We are fugitives, and the law is skinny with hunger for us.* I still wasn't asleep. So I said it again, and again, until the world turned fuzzy, nothing mattered, and I was gone.

Six

NO ONE CARED ABOUT THE POSTERS. NOT RIGHT AWAY. BUT *WE* cared. And that's why, the next morning, as soon as we were alone, we made three hundred more copies. The machine whirred and, with agonizing slowness, spit out copy after copy, the thing we had made together. The entire time, we touched the copier like we were laying hands on it, like it needed us for the miracle to happen.

As we drove around town, we tried to remember every single place we'd put up one of our posters. Had we put one on that particular telephone pole? Each time we saw one still up, we gasped, like they should have vaporized in direct sunlight. At the Creekside Market, while I posted one surreptitiously on the community bulletin board above the nightcrawlers and crickets, Zeke bought a detailed map of Coalfield, so we could mark every spot, to have an official record, to see how long some of them stayed up. It was the kind of obsession where, once we fell into it, we tried to be scientific, precise, but it was so warped by our desires that it wouldn't mean anything to anyone but us.

We drove over to the movie theater and an employee was taking down the wall of posters, his hands full of our art. I recognized the boy, one of my brothers' friends. So I rolled down the window and called out for him.

"Jake!" I said, and Zeke got very nervous.

"No," he said. "Don't draw attention to it. We have to be, like—"

"Jake!" I said again, and Jake, who was squinting at me, trying to place me within his world, finally nodded.

"Hey," he replied.

"What's all this?" I asked.

"I don't know," he said, shrugging. A wadded-up poster fell out of his hand and got caught in the wind. "My boss just told me to take 'em down. He's such a bitch. He called the cops to come look at it, but they said they didn't care."

"What are they?" I asked, so innocent. "Can I see one?"

"Frankie—" Zeke said.

Jake came over and showed us one. "It's kind of cool," he said. "I think it's, like, some metal band."

"Wow," I replied. "Pretty cool, definitely."

"I better get back to it," he finally said, after we all stared at the poster for a few seconds. "You want to keep one?" he asked.

"Sure," I said, and I handed the poster to Zeke, who just let it fall into his lap, stricken.

"Bye," Jake said, and he went back to ripping down the posters. I felt like, soon, we'd have to come right back to this spot and cover that wall again. If we didn't, I thought I'd burst into flames.

"He said his boss called the police," Zeke finally said as we drove away, in search of another one of our posters.

"Yeah," I replied, "but he said the cops didn't care."

Zeke thought about this, looked out the window. "They have no idea," he finally said.

"They're skinny with hunger for us," I said, and we both laughed, this weird, wobbly laugh. And we kept driving.

There was an abandoned house where I knew some kids went to smoke pot or drink at night, a place solitary enough that nobody really complained and the cops let it slide. I'd never been, but my brothers were there all the time with their girlfriends, with all those popular, effortless kids who did whatever they wanted. I didn't hate them. I didn't want to be them. But I had always been curious about how you could live a life where you never worried about repercussions, never considered that the thing you did rippled out into the world. That part seemed pretty great. So I thought, if Zeke and I couldn't be there at night, music blaring from a boom box, flashlights clicking on and off, cans of warm beer and crushed-up trucker speed passed around, then we'd put up our posters, force them to look at us.

The house seemed like it might cave in at any moment, broken glass everywhere. Who in the world would have sex in some abandoned house with this much broken glass on the ground? How did my brothers talk girls into it? And then there was the furniture: a moldy couch, a few recliners that looked like unspeakable things had been done to them, so many jagged slits in the fake leather. And I realized that, given the choice, it would be preferable to have sex on broken glass.

"This looks like a place where human sacrifices happen," Zeke said, looking worried.

"It's just teenager stuff," I said, trying to be cool. "I'm surprised it hasn't burned down because someone left a cigarette on the couch."

The walls in the living room, where most of the damage had occurred, were covered in Sharpie graffiti, the absolute dumbest shit, lots of dicks. Someone had tried to spray-paint the bird-flipping mascot from the Ugly Kid Joe album, but it looked like a Cabbage Patch Kid. I recognized the name of a girl I had been friends with in grade school. Someone had called her a bitch, and even though she had ditched me for more popular girls in junior high, I didn't like seeing her name for anybody to read. I grabbed a rock and scratched the wall over and over until you couldn't really read it anymore.

"Is this the edge?" Zeke asked me.

"I think that, maybe, everywhere we are is the edge," I said, mumbling at the end because I wasn't sure of myself. Honestly, I didn't want to think too much about it. I didn't want it to fall apart under scrutiny. I wanted it to just be there, the edge, the shantytown, the gold seekers. I wanted so badly to make it real.

"Let's cover the whole room," he said, reaching into his backpack.

"Yes, please," I said. "Let's do it."

And so we did.

It took longer than we thought, and every time rats scampered along the walls of the house, every creak as the foundation shifted, we startled and then looked to each other for reassurance. It took nearly two hundred copies of the poster, but we covered most of the room, and then we stood there, right in the center, and we turned slowly, around and around, and then it seemed like the whole world was just us, just this thing we'd made. It looked so close to what was in my brain that it took my breath away for a second. I thought about taking a picture of the room, to record it, but I just had my mind, my memory, and so I tried to hold it in there.

I knew that, with the broken windows, the holes in the ceiling, rain and damp and rot would get to the posters soon enough. I knew the next group of teenagers might tear it all down. I knew that it didn't really mean anything. But I wanted it to be there forever, so that when I was older, when I'd become the person I was going to be, I could come back and it would still be there. So that Zeke, if he ever went back to Memphis, and then went to some university in the Northeast, and then got married and had kids and started to forget about this summer, could come back to this house and it would all be here, and he would remember. And maybe, if we came back at the same time, all those years later, we'd remember each other.

Zeke found an empty but unbroken rum bottle and he rolled up one of our remaining posters and placed it inside the bottle, screwing the cap back on. He went over to the stairs, to a hole in the wall, and he dropped the bottle into it, where it clattered and settled inside the house, hidden away.

He looked at me, and I thought about the broken glass on the ground, how dirty my fingernails were, the cut on my finger that was probably infected now. I thought that if my first time with someone was in this house, I'd regret it. But I was so young. How did I know what I would and would not regret? Maybe I thought that I'd regret everything, that the key to my life was to hide inside my house, never talking to anyone, writing my stories in my notebook, and someday I'd believe that had been the right decision, that I hadn't ruined myself too quickly. But I wish I'd just done it, right then, ruined everything.

"I have to babysit tonight," I told him, checking my watch.

"Okay," he said, looking disappointed. He took the map out of his backpack and searched until he found the geographic location of this abandoned house and made a star with his pen. He held it open and we looked at the stars on the map. Even though Coalfield seemed like the dinkiest place on earth, when we counted the stars, all the open space that was still unmarked, I felt a little overwhelmed. I felt like maybe I wouldn't be able to sleep until the whole map was a single constellation.

I thought that the saddest thing that could happen was that something inside your head worked so hard to make it into the world and then nothing happened. It just disappeared. Now that I'd put those words into the open air, I needed them to multiply, to reproduce, to cover the world.

"Maybe just a few more stops on the way back home?" I offered, and this seemed to please Zeke.

"We can just use the rest of the copies," he said. He took one of the posters and folded it up, again and again, until it was a tiny square. He had to hold it closed with his fingers or it would open up again, expose itself. I wanted to eat it, but I didn't. I let him hold it in his hand, and then we walked out of the house. The sun was still in the sky, and it hurt my eyes. It made me want to hiss at it. We got into my car and Zeke held the map open, guiding us into so much territory left to chart.

THE NEXT MORNING, I AWAKENED FROM A DREAM WHERE THOSE giant hands from the poster, the ones Zeke had drawn, kept reaching out for me, the fingers wiggling like they were casting a spell of bad intentions over me. I moaned and groaned all the way into the kitchen, where my mom was eating yogurt at the counter, humming along to Tracy Chapman's "Give Me One Reason" and, like, really putting her hips into it. My brothers were inhaling Cookie Crisp in the living room, watching VHS tapes of an old SummerSlam pay-per-view on mute. I unwrapped my first Pop-Tart of the day, let the sugar seep into my gums, wake me up, my teeth aching.

I tried to imagine my dad back in this house with us, the summer sun so bright through the windows, the house just a little too hot because we were trying to save money on the A/C. But even though he'd only been gone for two years, I had trouble picturing him. Or maybe I tried not to. Because if I imagined him sitting in the easy chair in the living room the way he used to, I had to imagine his new wife, maybe making pancakes in the kitchen. And I had to imagine that other Frances, sucking on some melba toast, her disconcerting little baby fingers. It was strange, how his absence meant that I had to work hard to keep him out of my mind or else he took up too much space. I preferred to think that my dad was dead and his inheritance was coming to us in monthly installments, just enough to clothe and feed us.

I tried to imagine Zeke in the house, too, but he didn't make sense unless everyone else was gone. I could only picture him alone, on the couch, asking me to sit next to him. I finished my Pop-Tart, immediately wanted the second, but decided to save it for later. My mom looked up at me and smiled. "You look different," she said.

"I haven't combed my hair or anything," I said, feeling embarrassed.

"No," she said. "You just look happy."

"Oh, okay."

"I'm not used to seeing it, honestly," she told me. "It makes you look the tiniest bit crazy."

"Thanks, Mom."

"Will you see Zeke today?"

"Probably," I said, but, yeah, duh, of course I would see him.

"And do what?" she asked.

At that moment, I could feel something opening up in me and I realized how hard it was to walk through the day when you had an obsession and you couldn't say a word about it. I wanted to tell her that I was a fugitive, that it had happened so suddenly that I could scarcely believe it myself. I wanted to ask her if gold seekers were good or bad people. I wanted to ask her if she thought I was a gold seeker. I wanted to describe the feeling of pressing a single piece of paper against a brick wall, that little piece of duct tape trying to adhere to the rough surface, and how important it was for the tape to hold. I wanted to tell her that, maybe, if she made her own poster, and if she mailed it anonymously to my father, she would feel better. I wanted to tell her that I could breathe in time with the Xerox machine, that my insides felt like a copier. I wanted to ask if it was possible to have sex, to get it over with, without actually having sex. I wanted to ask her if my dad, when they first met, asked her to slice her finger and enact some weird blood oath. I wanted to show her my novel about the bad girl. I wanted to read it to her. And I wanted her to say, "This is so good, Frankie." And I'd say, "I don't feel like I belong here," and she'd say, "You mean Coalfield?" and I'd say, "Anywhere." My mouth was wide open. My mother had no idea what could come out of it.

"Hang out," I finally said. "Just, like, hang out."

She looked at me. If she brought up the condoms again, I would die. I wanted her to understand that there was something so much weirder inside of me, even if she didn't know exactly what it was.

"Well, have a great day," she said. She kissed me, collected her purse and keys, and left the kitchen. I reached for the other Pop-Tart and ate it in three bites.

"See ya, dum-dum," Charlie said, and my brothers rose, the whole house shifting to accommodate them, and they were off. I wished that I had two more of me. If there were three of us, three Frankies, maybe I'd stop vibrating so much, trying to keep it all in one stupid brain. I thought about that other Frances, my half sister. I decided that when she was a teenager, I'd show up at her school in a silver Porsche and kidnap her. I'd drive her to Coalfield. I'd show her one of my posters. And if she didn't understand, I'd drive her right back to my dad's house and kick her out of the car, not even slowing down.

And then, the rhythm of this summer giving me just enough time to wash my face and brush my teeth, Zeke was at my door, already sweating from the bike ride over. He had this jittery, nervous look about him, and he kind of pushed his way into the house.

"Your neighbor was really staring at me," he said. "He's kind of spooky. I think, maybe, he knows what we're doing. He had on, like, weird pajamas."

I walked out onto the porch and looked over at Mr. Avery, who waved. I waved back.

"It's not pajamas," I said, like that was the most important part of what Zeke had just told me, like it mattered at all. But it did to me. "It's a haori."

"What?" Zeke asked.

"It's like a kimono, but not so fancy. It's a kind of jacket, I think. He explained it to me once."

"Who is he?"

"Mr. Avery," I said. "He's from Los Angeles, but now he lives with his sister. He's neat. He used to be an artist. But he's pretty sick. That's why he wears the haori, because he says he's cold all the time."

"He was an artist?"

"Yeah, kind of. He tried to explain it to me once. It was, like, a performance. Performance art."

"I know about performance art . . . I think," Zeke replied.

"Well, that's what he did. In Los Angeles. And Japan, I think. That's where he got the haori. He's pretty proud of it."

"I think he knows what we're doing. He really stared at me."

"He's probably wondering what you're doing here, because I never have people come over. He's just bored. He's in the house all the time, except for these little walks that he takes around the block. He has cancer, I think. He's got other things to worry about than what we're doing."

I guess I should say that this was all before you could just google anyone and anything and actually get results. I had barely even used the internet at this point. And it wasn't like Randolph Avery was someone that you'd just know about if you were a teenager in Coalfield in the nineties. It wasn't until later that I realized who he was, how famous he had been. He was a hugely influential artist in the early eighties; he had pieces at MoMA, at LACMA. For the two years since he'd moved in with his sister, who was the postmaster in Coalfield, he was just Mr. Avery, this weird, sweet man who sometimes would talk to me with this faraway look on his face, like he had no idea how he'd ended up in this place.

"What did you do last night?" I asked Zeke.

"I mostly just drew in my notebook. There's not much else to do at my grandmother's house. She doesn't have cable or even a VCR. She just wants to play Uno all the time, so I do that for as long as I can stand it. The whole time, my mom is just playing her violin, which makes everything feel kind of creepy."

"She plays the violin? Like, in the same room as you?"

"Yeah, in the living room. She's just constantly playing, like me and my grandmother hired her to perform for us. And when she finishes a song, it's like, what do I do? Clap? Tell her that it's good? It doesn't matter anyway, because she just starts a new song. And then when she gets tired, she goes onto the front porch to smoke cigarettes, which she never did before."

"Yikes," I said. I thought about my mom, after my dad left us. For months, she had this stunned expression, like every five seconds she realized, once again, that this was all real, that she wasn't dreaming. And then one night at the dinner table I noticed that her shoulders weren't up around her ears, that her body was relaxed. Maybe she had met Hobart. Maybe she had realized that after all this time with my dad, it wasn't so bad to be without him. Whatever it was, she got loose. It made me happy. I wondered how long it would take for Zeke's mom. I wondered if it would ever happen.

"And then I go into my room and draw," Zeke continued. "I was working on this design. I was kind of thinking that maybe we should make another poster."

"Another one?" I said, stiffening.

"Yeah, like keep it going but also change things up a little. Like, can you think of something else you want to say on the poster?"

"No," I replied, feeling a little sad. "I already said it."

"I thought I could draw, like, a big wolf standing on a pile of bones. I sketched it out. Here, let me show you."

He got out his notebook and it was exactly like he explained, a big wolf on a pile of bones, but it didn't feel right. It didn't feel the same.

"I just . . . I don't want to do another one," I finally said, after he pointed to the wolf, like I hadn't seen it, like I didn't realize that the figure on top of the bones was a big fucking wolf.

"You don't ever want to make anything else?" he said, and I could feel him slipping away from me a little, and I needed to pull him back.

"I want to make stuff forever, for as long as I live. But I want our poster to be the only one we make. It's special. It's the first one we made. It's perfect, right? It's perfect. It has our blood on it."

"We could bleed on this," he said, pointing to the wolf again.

"Do you know what I mean, Zeke?" I asked, and the whole world depended on what he said. I got one of the copies of our poster, and I held it out for him. "This is what the world gets. If we do more, lots of different designs, new words, we'll lose it. It just goes away. It's like . . . I don't know . . . ordinary. Do you know what I mean?"

He looked at the poster, and I watched as his lips formed the words that I had written. He smiled. And then he nodded and looked up at me.

"Yeah," he said. "I know what you mean. Okay. Just this. Only this."

"Only this," I said, and we walked into the garage, over to the copier, to make more.

Seven

OVER THE NEXT FOUR DAYS, HERE ARE A FEW OF THE PLACES IN Coalfield where we put the posters: on the bulletin board of the public library; folded up in forty-six random books in the stacks of the library; on the inside door of the stalls in the men's and women's bathrooms of the Golden Gallon gas station; on the back of every box of Cookie Crisp cereal in the Kroger; all over the gazebo in Marcia Crooks Park; the back wall of the movie theater (again); in the mailboxes of 270 residences in town; on the dumpster behind the Hardee's; in the pocket of someone's jeans in an unlocked locker at the public pool; across the entire front window of the hair salon that had gone out of business a few months earlier; in the comment box of the Wendy's; in a shoebox for a pair of size 6 sneakers at Payless; taped to the flagpole in front of Coalfield High School; in an envelope without a return address, mailed to the *Coalfield Ledger*; on the car windshield of a pastor who tried to get sex ed abolished from the high school curriculum; on the bulletin board of Spinners Tapes and CDs, which sold glass pipes and incense and was glowing inside from black lights; under a bunch of Dilly Bars in the freezer of the Dairy Queen; on the gravestone of the last Confederate soldier in Coalfield.

On the map, there were so many stars, it made me dizzy to look at it.

There were so many stars that, now, other people couldn't help but notice. They couldn't help but see the image, the words, and wonder, "What *is* this?"

I was upstairs in my room, writing my novel. It was weird, but having made the poster, having put it up everywhere, I felt like something had been unlocked in my brain. I couldn't stop writing the novel about the evil Nancy Drew. I was now at the point where her sister, Tess, the dumb girl detective, stumbles onto a piece of evidence that their father, the police chief, had previously ignored, a piece of evidence that Evie had accidentally left behind and that could incriminate her. And now Evie was trying to convince her sister that the evidence didn't mean anything, was worthless, that it would waste everyone's time. Evie was reaching out for the evidence, waiting for Tess to give it up, Evie's hand just hovering there, inches from Tess's own hand, so close that they could shock each other with just the slightest charge. And what was weird, as I wrote, trying to get it all down, was that I really didn't know if Tess would give it to her.

And then my brothers clomped into the house, and it broke my concentration. I realized how hungry I was, and sometimes the triplets brought home leftover burgers, cold fries, so I went downstairs to see if they had anything, even though I knew it would make me sick. Zeke was out grocery shopping with his grandmother, and he had promised to see if the posters were still stuck to the boxes of Cookie Crisp.

When I stepped into the living room, my brothers were sitting on the sofa, leaning over the coffee table, staring at a copy of the poster. My poster.

"What's . . . what's that?" I asked, my voice sticking in my throat, like it hurt to ask.

"What does it look like, dum-dum?" Andrew said.

"I don't know," I replied.

"Well, neither do we," Andrew said.

"They're all over town," Charlie said. "I found a bunch of them taped up to the dumpster."

"And Jenna said her parents got one in their mailbox," Brian said.

"It's kind of fucked up," Andrew said.

"It seems like something you guys would do," I finally said.

"Yeah, I know," Charlie replied. "But we didn't."

"What. Is. IT?" Brian said, clearly frustrated, like the poster was infecting his brain.

"Like, is it a band?" Charlie said. "Fugitives? That's a stupid fucking name for a band."

"Look at those goddamn hands!" Brian shouted.

Just then my mom came home from work. She was holding one of the posters. "Boys," she said, the poster flapping around in her hand like an unruly bird, "did you do this?"

"NO!" all three of my brothers shouted in unison.

"Oh, thank god," my mom replied, sagging against the door for a second. "Hobart is writing an article about it."

Hobart was a guy who worked at the local newspaper. My mom pretended that he was only a friend, but we all knew that they'd been dating in secret, off and on for the last four months. My mom would feel overwhelmed or worry they were getting too close, say they couldn't see each other, and then they'd end up at Gilly's Bar and Grill, dancing to the J. Geils Band on the jukebox. They had known each other in high school, though they hadn't been romantic, but I think my mom needed someone who wasn't my dad, like maybe the complete opposite. Hobart had this scruffy, unkempt beard and wore Hawaiian shirts and talked about the movie *Billy Jack* all the time. He was like if Lester Bangs wrote about Fourth of July cake contests instead of the Stooges. And I was happy that there was a guy, even if he was a little embarrassing to me, that my mom could look at and think, *Maybe you'll be better than the last guy*. Hobart seemed like a good dude to start with. And now he was going to write about our poster.

"What do you mean, he's going to write about it?" I asked. "What is there to say?"

"Well, you know, it's kind of a mystery, all these posters spread out across the town. He figures it's a bunch of teenagers just messing around, but he said it's pretty sophisticated. He says he's pretty sure that the quote is by a French poet named Rimbaud. He thinks the art is from some underground comic."

"Rimbaud?" I said. "Leonardo DiCaprio played him in that movie."

"Well, there you go," my mom said, satisfied. "Teenagers love Leo, so they probably started reading a bunch of Rimbaud."

"That's not what teenagers do, Mom," Charlie said.

"Well, it's all just a theory right now," my mom said, already moving on, so happy that her boys weren't responsible.

I looked over at the triplets, all three of them mouthing the words on the poster, their hands hovering just above the drawings. "What are all these dots?" Andrew asked.

"Stars," I said. "They look like stars."

MAZZY BROWER

MAZZY CALLED ME AGAIN, THIS TIME WHILE I WAS ALONE IN THE house, folding laundry, always folding laundry, my daughter going through four pairs of socks a day, stripping them off and tossing them behind the sofa, under the bed, and I was forever washing them, drying them, rolling them into balls, placing them in her dresser, until she would do it all over again. The phone rang, and, like an idiot, I picked up.

"Frankie?" she said, getting my name right.

"Oh, no," I said. "No, thank you."

"Just wait. I want to talk for just a few seconds."

"I don't want to talk, though," I said.

"But you answered the phone, right? Do you think maybe you wanted me to call you again? Do you think maybe it might be good to talk to someone about it?"

"First, I *did not* want you to call again. Second, it *would not* be good to talk to someone about it. Third . . ."

"Yes?"

"I actually don't have a third thing. I am just very afraid of you and this story."

"It doesn't have to be like this, though," she continued. "I know parts of the story, but you know all of it. That's what I want to talk to you about. I want to get a sense of how this came to be. I want to know how you did it. Why you did it. And what you think about it now."

"I don't know how to answer any of that," I told her.

"I think you do," she said. "I think maybe this is something you think about a lot."

"Well . . . yes. That's true. But I still don't know how I'd answer any of those questions."

"That's okay. I'd just love to meet, to talk, one-on-one. Off the record at first, even. Whatever you want."

I could feel the world getting smaller and smaller, and that scared me because I'd already made myself pretty small to ensure none of these memories got out of me. To have the larger world shrinking down made it worse, to know that people were searching for you.

"I have to go," I said.

"Frankie," she tried, just as I was hanging up, "I think you need to talk about this. People died. It's . . . it's a big deal."

"I'm sorry," I said.

And the memories sped up even more. And that made me angry, that they were moving too fast for me to even recognize those moments. I sat on the sofa. The room smelled fresh, like fabric softener, and I closed my eyes and I willed the memories to slow down. I made them go at the exact speed as it happened then, like I was stepping right back into it, and I promised myself that I wouldn't let it get away from me.

Eight

THE NEXT DAY, I PICKED UP ZEKE AND WE DROVE AROUND TOWN. Zeke was playing a cassette he'd brought from Memphis, a mix by someone named DJ Squeeky, this slowed-down voice saying, over and over, "Burn, baby, burn, baby, burn, baby, burn." It felt hypnotic, the way the whole world seemed wavy and shimmery, the windows down, the heat oppressive, and then we'd see another one of our posters, and everything would speed up for a second. My backpack was filled with more copies, but Zeke was worried, afraid that we'd get caught. We put a few in mailboxes of houses that were obviously empty, marking the spots on the map, but mostly we just drove.

I'd never felt particularly connected to Coalfield; I mean, I felt *anchored* to it, like the years I'd spent here would make it harder for me to live anywhere else, but I never felt shaped by it. Everyone thinks the South is, like, Flannery O'Connor.

They think it's haunted. And maybe it is, deep down, in the soil, but I never saw it that way. We had a McDonald's. I don't know how else to say it. There was no bookstore, okay, fine. The museums we had were of the Old Jail Museum or Military Vehicle Museum or Railroad Museum variety. We had a Wal-Mart. I wore normal clothes. And as I drove Zeke around my town, I pointed out things like "I fell off that merry-go-round and knocked out a baby tooth," or "That shoe store is eighty years old and if you buy a pair of shoes, you can put a wooden coin in this machine and a mechanical chicken will poop out a plastic egg that has candy in it," or "I stole a heavy metal magazine at that Bi-Lo because I wanted a poster of Lita Ford for my room." I felt like maybe I kind of loved the place. Or, no, I just wanted Zeke to love it. And if he didn't, if the old-timey pharmacy where you could get cherry limeades didn't impress him, I'd tape one of our posters under the counter and then how could he not feel something like love for it?

While we made seven consecutive loops around the town square, Zeke told me that his grandmother had heard about the posters at her Bible study meeting the night before. Some old lady had found one and brought it to the meeting. "They all think it's got something to do with the devil," Zeke said. "Devil worship, something like that." One of the ladies was convinced that the words were a play on a verse from Revelation, so they spent the whole class trying to locate it, poring over the Bible, never finding what they wanted.

"Everyone thinks it's from something," I said.

"Everything is, kinda, from something," he replied.

"Well, duh, but this is from me. Just me."

"And me," he said, smiling.

"And you."

At the Creekside Market, we bought two bottles of Sun Drop and a handful of grape bubble gum. We checked the bulletin board and our poster was still there. When I stared at it, the poster turned wavy, like a mirage. I reached into my book bag, and when the guy working the counter looked away, I put up another poster, right on top of the other one. I felt the aura double, maybe quadruple, and I got a little dizzy. I drank half of the Sun Drop right there, standing in the market, just glug-glug-glug like I was dying of thirst, and then I stumbled outside, into the heat. This was the beauty of obsession, I realized. It never waned. Real obsession, if you did it right, was the same intensity every single time, a kind of electrocution that kept your heart beating in time. It was so good.

Zeke was waiting outside for me, and we clinked our bottles together. He reached into my bag, grabbed another poster, and folded it into a paper airplane. He waited a few seconds to make sure no one was watching us, and he flicked it toward an empty car in the parking lot whose windows were down. It caught the wind, sailed toward the window, and we held our breath at how perfect it was, and then the paper plane did some weird loop-de-loop and crashed to the ground. Zeke quickly crab-walked over to the paper airplane and chucked it through the open window, into the passenger seat, and we giggled. Zeke grabbed my arm and pulled me closer, and we kissed. But I hadn't been entirely ready and our teeth clicked together and that made me hiss a little, thinking I'd cracked one of my front teeth. I wanted to try again right away, now that I was expecting it, but I was afraid that I'd still ruin it, like somehow I'd end up biting his nose off.

It was our first kiss in public, which, to my mind, made it official. I didn't know *what* was official, what we were announcing. We weren't dating. He wasn't my boyfriend, or I didn't think of him that way, not truly. I looked around to see if anyone had noticed, like maybe they could tell us what all of this meant, but we were invisible. We didn't matter. So I kissed him again. That's what was official, that we were invisible to everyone in the entire world except each other.

A lady banged the door of the market open and came out with a handful of Little Debbie snack cakes. She was heading right to the car that now had one of our posters in the passenger seat. We hopped into my car and drove off, not looking back to see what would happen.

And the whole summer might have continued in this way. It's so easy to imagine. We'd hang posters, and people would get tired of the mystery, and we'd settle into the heat. I'd have sex with Zeke, the most painless sex possible, under the covers in my little bed, using the condom my mother had said was nonnegotiable. His mom would finally realize either that she wanted to reconcile with her husband or that she needed a job now that she was a single mom, and they'd move back to Memphis. And I'd hold him in my mind, that one summer. We'd send each other our art, his drawings and my novel. We'd write occasional letters until real life intruded, college applications, new friends. Every other Thanksgiving, he'd come back to Coalfield to see his grandmother and we'd drive around town and maybe we'd even hang up a few of the posters, just to feel that thrill again. We'd make out in my car. We'd graduate from college and he'd end up on one side of the country and I'd be on the other. And I'd publish my novel, and at a bookstore in Denver, Colorado, he'd be in the audience. We'd get coffee and maybe have sex in my hotel room, even though he was married now. I'd write a book about that one summer. He'd leave his wife and seven children, and we'd get married in our late fifties, and we'd frame that first poster and hang it in our living room.

But none of that happened, did it? And I still don't know if that makes me happy or sad.

THE DAY AFTER WE'D GONE TO THE CREEKSIDE MARKET, BILLY Curtis (everybody in school called him Sunshine Billy Curtis because he was always sunburned) and Brooke Burton didn't come home from a night out, and their parents called the cops. And at 10 A.M. on Saturday, before the cops had even really started thinking about looking for them, they showed up on the front porch of the Curtis house, disheveled and hungover and looking like shit. And they said something terrible had happened, that they had met the fugitives.

What they told the police, as the two of them stood on the porch, their heads hammering from the alcohol they had been drinking all night, was that they had been walking to go visit some friends and maybe watch a video when a black van pulled up beside them. There was a man and a woman in the front of the van, wearing all black, covered in tattoos. They asked Billy and Brooke to join them, and when Billy asked where they were going, the man said, "To the edge." And then the back door opened and another man, also wearing all black, jumped out and grabbed Brooke and pulled her into the van. Billy jumped in to save her, and someone in the front knocked him out. They knocked out Brooke, too.

When they woke up, they were at this abandoned house, one they'd never seen before, far from civilization, out in the woods. There were candles everywhere, and the walls were covered in these strange posters that had these menacing hands. The three people, who called themselves *the fugitives*, were listening to strange, satanic music, and were doing all manner of drugs. They made Brooke and Billy do drugs, like they, I don't know, shoved them up their noses or blew smoke into their faces? It wasn't entirely clear. And the intensity of these drugs made Brooke and Billy pass out again. And when they woke up in the morning, the three people were gone. And so Billy and Brooke walked all the way home, constantly worried that the fugitives would come back for them. Each of them had brought a copy of the poster home with them, for evidence.

I learned all of this from the triplets, who recounted the entire thing to me and my mom over lunch that afternoon. And my mom, to her credit, said, "Oh god, they made it up, right?" and my brothers told us what had really happened, since they had actually been at the abandoned house that night and had the sense to get back home in time to avoid having the cops search for them. They didn't even hesitate in the telling, however it might incriminate them, because my mom knew all this and worse about her sons, but she also knew that they were the most invincible children in the entire state.

Billy and Brooke had gone to party with some of their friends. And they were at the abandoned house, drinking rum punch and smoking weed and maybe doing some crushed-up speed. And they went out into the woods to have sex and their friends forgot about them and drove home around three in the morning. And Billy and Brooke passed out. And when they woke up and saw that it was morning, they knew they were fucked. They'd be grounded for the rest of the summer. They walked back to the abandoned house, saw all the posters, which they'd laughed at the night before. Someone had been tearing them off the walls and setting them on fire. But they were at least five miles from home and their parents were probably freaking out.

And I could see it so clearly, the house, because Zeke and I had been there and had put those posters on the walls. And I knew that they were just the dumbest kids, trying anything to avoid punishment, but I chose to believe that the poster, because of how beautiful it was, how strange it was, had opened up some little part of their brain, and it gave them a story that would put them in danger even though they thought it would keep them safe.

And then Hobart came over, a few minutes before I was supposed to meet up with Zeke, and he was red-faced and breathless. He said he'd been at the "scene of the crime" and that the police had used the entire fiscal year's caution tape budget on this single house. He said his source in the department, who I knew was Brandon Pinkleton, because there were only five officers and he was the youngest and most desperate to seem important, said that they believed it was a credible threat and they had put out an APB to the surrounding counties to be on the lookout for a black van with three individuals with black hair and multiple tattoos with satanic symbology.

"It's not real," my mom said, and I could see Hobart deflate a little, like he had been waiting for someone to say it, but he instantly puffed back up, his Hawaiian shirt expanding, the little palm trees swaying. "Well, now, the police are saying it's a credible threat, okay? And, you know, I've been looking at those posters all over town, and it feels like maybe the beginnings of what you might call psychological terrorism. That's the angle right now."

"The angle?" I asked, trying to act like I didn't care.

"For the newspaper," he replied. "I think someone, and I believe they're outsiders, possibly connected to some kind of cult, are using Coalfield as the initial test subject for something pretty downright scary."

"Dude, come on," Charlie said, "Sunshine made this shit up. It's complete and total, like, what do you call it? Frankie? What do you call it?"

"Fiction?" I guessed.

"Yeah, right. It's fiction," Charlie said.

"Well, I'm reporting what the facts are, okay?" Hobart replied, starting to get some traction in the face of skepticism, which is how almost every bad idea gets worse. "I've got some disturbing imagery and sloganeering that has suddenly appeared in town. I've got two youths reporting that they were abducted by some kind of cult and forced to do drugs. I've got . . . well, that's all I've got right now. That's newsworthy, though."

"Is it?" my mom asked. I could see on her face that this was one of the moments when she wondered why she sometimes dated this man.

"It is for Coalfield," Hobart replied.

I finally turned to see Zeke, standing in the doorway, and I had no idea how long he'd been there, but the look on his face made me think that he'd heard Hobart say the words "disturbing imagery."

"Zeke," I said quietly, almost to myself, but my mom saw him, too.

"Hey," Zeke said. "What's . . . um . . . what's going on?"

"There's some kind of weird drug cult in Coalfield," Andrew said.

"A sex cult," Charlie offered.

"A satanic sex drug cult," Brian clarified.

"In Coalfield?" Zeke asked.

"Oh, Zeke," my mom said, "it's nothing like that. Don't be scared."

"Well, I mean, I'm not scared. It's just . . . well, it's the first I'm hearing about this. I'm new to the area, you know? I'm just here for the summer, and so I'm not exactly, like, privy to the news in this town."

I realized that if Zeke stayed in this room with Hobart for more than five minutes, he would produce hundreds of copies of our poster, pulling them like a magic trick from the pockets of his jean shorts, admitting everything, convincing himself that, somehow, he was the leader of this satanic-drug-sex cult. I knew that he was jumpy, had some anxiety. I had it, too, but I think I'd had a head start on unhappiness, on being disappointed by people who supposedly loved you, and so I had settled into it a little more. I did not feel guilt for the weird things inside of me anymore. I was a fugitive, and I was not ready to be caught yet.

In my room, the door closed, I looked at Zeke for any signs of instability. "Are you okay?" I asked him. He had this faraway look in his eyes, like he was running simulations of how his life was going to turn out.

"Yeah, I mean, of course," he finally replied. "It's just . . . well, I don't like the fact that the police are involved."

"Okay, you're from Memphis, so I get it, but this is Coalfield and the cops are idiots, okay? They think three random headbangers grabbed Sunshine Billy Curtis and his girlfriend and *made* them do drugs."

"Yeah, I get it. But, like, that's worse. Them being so stupid is what's scary because now it's this whole *thing*."

"We wanted it to be a *thing*, though, right?"

"Not a *thing* that ended up with you and me in jail," he said. "I wanted it to be more like a *thing* where somebody puts the poster on a skateboard deck in a few years."

"Well, that's better, yeah. That is more what I'd wanted, too. But we made it, right? We made the poster. So we can still control it, I think."

"I don't think that's how art works," he said, unsure of himself, which was disconcerting because, even though Zeke had always been kind of nervous, he'd always seemed really self-assured about what he thought he knew about the world.

"Okay, well, maybe we take a day or two off. We wait and see what happens," I said.

"A *day?*" he said, almost shouting.

"Or *two*, okay? I said *a day or two.*"

"And then what?" he asked.

"We keep putting up the posters," I said, like, *duh*, of course that's what we do.

"I don't want to get arrested for a fucking poster," Zeke said, starting to shake a little.

It stung me a little to hear him talk about the poster like that. Like, I know that I was the crazier one, the more broken one, but that summer, what I'd written, what Zeke had drawn, what we'd bled all over, it was the most important thing in the world to me. I would have gone to jail for the poster. I think I would have killed someone if they tried to keep me from putting up the poster. Because if it stopped, what was next? Zeke would leave. I'd never see him again. I'd go back to school, invisible, sad. My dad would never come back. My brothers would all move away. My mom would marry Hobart. It wasn't really that bad, I know. It was life. But I didn't want life right then. I wanted the summer, that poster. I wanted the edge, the shantytown, the gold seekers. I had said it. I said *we are fugitives*. I had meant it, even though I didn't know what it meant. And now, maybe, we were. I wanted Zeke to understand. The hands that he had drawn, hovering over the children, never actually touched them, couldn't reach them. How could he not see that?

I leaned into him, reached for his backpack. I got out his notebook, all those strange little drawings. "What are you—" he said, but I just shook my head. He made an ineffectual gesture toward the notebook, trying to protect it, but

I carried it over to my desk. I reached into the drawer and produced what I had of my novel. I slammed it down on the bed, which was also really ineffectual, not the sound that I'd hoped for.

"This is my novel," I said.

"I know," he replied.

"Read it," I said. "I'm going to let you read it."

"Okay," he said. "Do you want, like, suggestions, or—"

"I do not want comments or suggestions, no," I replied. "Just read it. And I'm going to look at your drawings."

"You've seen most of them already," he said. "And you've told me a lot about your book."

"We'll do this for maybe an hour, and then we'll decide what to do next," I told him.

I lay down on the bed, and Zeke scooted over to me. I looked at a drawing of a landscape, but drawn in sections, like an ant farm, and in one of the underground tunnels, there was a fire burning.

"I like this," I said. "This is new."

"Thank you. This is a really good first line," he said.

"Thank you."

And we lay like that, absorbing the thing that mattered to the other person. And then I said, "Zeke? It's okay, all right?"

"Okay, I believe you."

After a second, Zeke added, "Please don't say the line. Just not right now. I know it. I think about it all the time. You don't have to tell me."

"Okay," I said.

And that hour in the room, the two of us almost touching, the thing we made beginning to fully assemble itself, to spread out into the world, was the happiest I have maybe ever been in my entire life.

THE FRONT-PAGE HEADLINE OF THE NEXT DAY'S EDITION OF THE *Coalfield Ledger* read EVIL COMES TO COALFIELD. My mom yelled at Hobart, and he said that he'd originally had a question mark at the end, but the editor changed it. "If it's interrogative, you know, it's really not that irresponsible," he said. When I rolled my eyes, he said, "And, by the way, sometimes it's the role of the journalist to be provocative."

"At the *Coalfield Ledger*?" my mom shouted.

The front page also had two images. The first was a color photograph of the abandoned house where Billy and Brooke had been "held captive," and it really did look like the cops had accidentally unspooled a dozen rolls of police tape and, instead of rolling it all back up, had just decided to hang it on anything in the vicinity of the possible crime scene. The second image was a reproduction of our poster, which honestly looked kind of fuzzy and unthreatening on the crappy newsprint. It had been reduced in size so you couldn't really make out the phrase, but I still found myself silently mouthing along to it as I stared.

Hobart hadn't even talked to Billy and Brooke because their parents said they needed privacy in order to recover from the shock of the experience. He had made a three-minute phone call to a retired professor of criminal justice at ETSU, who said that the poster was interesting because hands were not a typical symbol in satanic graffiti, although the children certainly complicated things. He said he'd need to spend more time with the words on the poster, look at the mathematical possibilities for converting the letters into numbers that might connect with 666. He said it also might be lyrics from a heavy metal song, which was typical for graffiti of this nature. He said his last real work had been on the prevalence of the occult in unsolved murder cases in the eighties, so he felt certain he might find some linkages to this poster.

"A reporter from Nashville is coming today to follow up on the story," Hobart said.

"About a poster?" my mom asked, dumbfounded.

"About the possible implications of the poster," Hobart clarified.

"This is stuff that people disproved a decade ago, Hobart," my mom said. "Tipper Gore? Hobart, do you want to be like Tipper freaking Gore?"

"That's different and you know it," he told her. "Dungeons and Dragons and, I don't know, Judas Priest, of course that's bullshit. But there's no source for this, okay? It's a mystery."

It suddenly dawned on me that it was eight thirty in the morning and Hobart was standing in our living room in the clothes he had worn the day before. That was more troubling to me than getting caught, that my mom had somehow drawn Hobart closer just as he was messing up the one thing that I cared about.

ZEKE SHOWED UP AT MY HOUSE THAT AFTERNOON WITH HIS grandmother's copy of the newspaper.

"I can't tell you how much I hate your mom's boyfriend," he said, and I instantly clarified that my mom was proudly single, an independent woman, and Hobart was just an acquaintance.

"Well, he's going to ruin our lives," Zeke said, and it didn't sound all that histrionic. I mean, our lives were built around hanging up the poster, putting it everywhere in Coalfield, and Hobart had temporarily derailed that. But I knew, even then, that Zeke was talking about something else. He meant when his real life started again. He was worried that he'd have a juvenile record and he might not get into art school or something like that. His dad might disown him. Adults would be disappointed. There was this tiny little separation between us. We were bound together; we had made something. But now that it was real, that other people noticed, I knew that I had to reach out and hold on to Zeke or it would disappear.

I grabbed my bag, filled with posters, and we got into my car. And we just drove, up and down streets with rows of sad, plain houses with maybe one or two that were nice. You could imagine the town going one way or the other so easily, that the crappy houses would get torn down and new ones put up, or those fancy houses would fall apart, would fade, and then all the houses would be empty. I told Zeke to get out the map from the glove compartment, and he did, reluctantly. He was suddenly treating everything as *evidence* now. He didn't say it, but I knew he was thinking about fingerprints, which was laughable to me. We were ghosts. No one could see us. Why did it matter if they found little swirls on a poster? Who cared about fingerprints? Focus on the shantytowns, you morons. Look at that.

And we ticked off spots we'd hit. Some were still there, which was one of the most satisfying feelings you can imagine, but others were gone. I wanted to replace them, but Zeke said it was too soon, that someone might be watching. He had one of the posters in his lap, and he started folding it and refolding it. I thought he was doing origami, that soon he'd be holding a little swan, but he really was just reducing the poster to the smallest possible square that he could, as if, by the force of his anxiety, he could fold the poster so many times that it simply disappeared, ceased to exist. I stopped the car at a car wash and made sure that no one was around.

"Do you feel bad about the poster?" I asked. "Why are you so upset?"

"It's not the poster. Like, well, you know, I love the poster. I think it's cool. It's just, I'm really scared because nobody else seems to understand it."

"I guess I kind of thought that we didn't want anyone else to understand it, right? Like, it's just us. We're the only ones who know what it is."

He thought about it for a second. "I mean, yeah," he continued, "but, like, I kind of wanted other people to not understand it in ways that they assumed a really cool artist had made it. I didn't want them to not understand it in a way that they think we're devil worshippers who abduct kids."

"But it's *not* that. Whatever they think, we know what it really is," I told him.

"I'm just—" he said, but then started staring out the window. I thought maybe a police cruiser had pulled into the parking lot, but the coast was clear.

"Here, just, like, give me that poster," I said, and I took the folded-up poster he was still holding. I smoothed it out on my lap. "I'm just going to hang this up. We'll feel a ton better if you can see me hang it up and, you know, we don't get arrested on the spot. And then maybe I'll put up a few more. There's a lot in the bag, and we'll just see where that takes us."

"There's one up," he said, now pointing at the change machine built into the brick wall at the front of the unmanned car wash station.

"Well, like, we can put up more," I said. "That's no big deal. Or somewhere else. Whatever."

He grabbed the map and held it up for me. "We never put a poster here," he said.

"Yeah, no, I think we did," I said.

"No, we never put one here," he said, pointing at the spot on the map, pristine, unmarked.

"Maybe I did?" I offered.

"Did you?" he asked, his voice cracking just a bit.

"I don't know. I don't remember doing it. Maybe in my sleep?"

"Frankie, seriously, did you put up that poster?" he asked.

"I don't think so."

We both got out of the car and walked over to the change machine. *The edge is a shantytown.* The hands. Our blood, speckles of it. It was our poster. I stared at it. But it wasn't our poster. I pulled it off the machine, and I noticed immediately that the paper was not the crappy discount copy paper we had in the garage. It was nicer. Fancier. A little more weight and heft. The color was pristine white, too, not the yellow tint of our posters. We walked back to my car, and I checked it against the copy I'd taken from Zeke.

"Oh, well, okay, that's . . . it's not ours," I finally said.

"Then whose is it?" he asked.

"I don't know. Somebody took one of our posters and made more copies, I guess."

"They made copies?"

"I guess, Zeke! Jesus, I don't know."

Zeke thought about this for a second. The idea that someone else might get credit for the poster seemed to alarm him, but the idea that someone else might get the electric chair for making the posters seemed to temporarily assuage his anxiety. "So they stole it?" he finally asked.

"I don't know how it works," I admitted. "Is it stealing to make a copy of it? I mean, we made copies of it. We have the original. We made it. Someone else is just, like, sharing it."

"Why, though?" Zeke asked.

"Because it's awesome," I reminded him. "We made it and people like it, or at least someone likes it. So they're making sure other people see it."

"I guess I just didn't think about this," he said.

"We're okay, Zeke," I said. "Nothing is going to happen to us. Nothing bad, at least."

He took our copy of the poster, smoothed it out again, and then reached into the backpack for the tape. All by himself, he walked back to the change machine and put up our copy of the poster. He looked at me, still watching him from the car, and he gave me a thumbs-up. And we drove around Coalfield, and we didn't come home until the backpack was empty.

A FEW DAYS LATER, THE *TENNESSEAN* RAN AN ARTICLE IN THE Local News section that had the headline TROUBLING STREET

ART VEXES SMALL TOWN. The article itself reasserted the concerns that the art was in some way related to some heretofore unknown cult. Whether it was a local chapter of a national cult or a homegrown one, the reporter could not definitively say. A lawyer for Billy and Brooke (Brooke's uncle, who only did personal injury lawsuits and had a radio commercial that said, "If you've been wronged, I'll make it right") provided an official statement that the two upstanding youths were now unsure of the validity of the exact details within their original statement, possibly due to unknowingly ingesting psychedelic drugs. They did, however, stand by the assertion that three people, who called themselves "fugitives" or "the fugitives," had abducted them. A Methodist preacher was quoted as saying that the King James Bible had only a few references to fugitives (or a word synonymous with *fugitive*) and "none of them are particularly pleasant." The reporter mentioned that the local police force had noted a rash of calls from concerned citizens who had seen a black van or mysterious figures dressed in black, but nothing had come of the subsequent investigations. An art professor at Watkins College said the poster had "echoes of street graffiti popular in large cities like New York and Philadelphia" and that the creators seemed to have some awareness of culturally relevant artists like Jean-Michel Basquiat and Keith Haring. When asked about the possibility of occult imagery in the poster, the professor offered, "I mean, sure, that's definitely in there, too."

I had no idea who Basquiat was. I'd seen some Keith Haring artwork in a magazine somewhere, but I didn't think what we'd made looked anything like that, weirdo big-headed dancing figures. It made me a little angry. It was a small thing, but

I wanted to know if the professor thought the poster was any good.

In the final paragraph, the reporter quoted Teddie Cowan, the county sheriff, saying, "Now is not the time to panic, but, also, there seem to be dark forces at play, and I will do everything in my power as an upholder of justice to root them out and send them as far from Coalfield as is humanly possible."

And though I was alone in the house, my family all at work, I could see Zeke in my mind, a true vision of him. He was standing on my front porch, holding a copy of this newspaper in his hand, waiting for me to tell him that everything was okay, that we were not in trouble. And I would tell him that, the minute I opened the door and saw him, his weird mouth, his big eyes. I'd immediately tell him that this was a good thing. We'd made something good. I'd tell him that we were invincible, that nothing bad would ever happen to either one of us. And I'd tell him that the only thing that we could do, because there really was no other choice, was to put up more of the posters. The only way to keep ourselves safe, I would tell him, was to make more of them.

Nine

A HEAT WAVE HAD ROLLED IN, AND I WAS SWEATING CONstantly, from, well, obviously, the actual heat, but also from the wild feeling that things were quickly moving beyond my control. I was trying to figure out how to keep everything from falling apart, to hold on to this thing that I'd made, but that was getting harder and harder. And so I was perpetually red-faced, itchy, my shirts soaked with sweat. My whole mouth felt electric. My stomach hurt all the time, and to deal with it, I just ate more Pop-Tarts and Cheetos Puffs, and that made it worse. I'd written fifty pages of the novel in a week; I could not stop. I needed a story that I could control, that wouldn't keep going when I stopped writing it.

When I say the posters were everywhere, I mean that we were not the only people in possession of the poster. And I don't just mean Coalfield, although the town was now covered in the thing that Zeke and I had made, the posters like a swarm of cicadas, sticking to everything.

We were eating dinner one night, watching channel 4, and the host, who had come back to Tennessee after serving as the sidekick for, I shit you not, Pat Sajak's disaster of a talk show, was talking about the poster. And my mom said, "Oh my god, I cannot believe this. Hobart is going to be . . . just the worst."

The host mentioned Coalfield, and there was some footage of our town, the square, our poster, but then there were videos of the streets of Nashville, a row of the posters flapping in the wind. And I noticed, even from that distance, that it wasn't really our poster. First, it was on bright orange paper, which I thought made it look spooky in a silly way, like Halloween. But, also, the hands were different, less detailed. The whole poster lacked detail. It looked, honestly, like shit. Some reporter on the street was now holding one of the posters up for the camera, which focused on it, and the second half of the phrase read, "we are the New Fugitives," and I thought, *What the hell is that?*

"That's not right," I said out loud, and my mom looked at me.

"What's not right?" she asked.

"It's just . . . I mean, the line is different from the ones in Coalfield."

"Oh," she said, squinting at the TV. "It looks right to me. Gold seekers? Shantytown?"

"The edge is a shantytown filled with gold seekers—"

"No, I know, Frankie," she said, but I just kept going, "—we are *fugitives* and the law is skinny with hunger for us."

"Okay," my mom said.

"Skinny with hunger," Andrew said, already on his third bowl of Hamburger Helper. "Skinny with hunger. I like that. Skinny with hunger."

"I do, too," I said, not even looking over at him, "but that said *new fugitives*, and . . . well, that's not what the poster says."

"Well, that's what *that* poster says," Charlie offered.

"Yeah . . . ," I replied, not sure how to explain. Or, no, I knew how to explain, but I also knew that I couldn't really do it.

AND IT WAS STRANGE, BUT AS I STARTED TO GET MAD, ZEKE seemed lighter, more calm. To his mind, the fact that there was at least one other person in Coalfield putting up the posters made it easier for us to deny our involvement. Even if we got caught, we were just stupid kids trying to imitate what we'd seen. We were so impressionable. So stupid. So desperate. We just wanted to be cool because we were so uncool, and you're not going to call our parents are you, Officer?

Needless to say, I did not care for this at all. I would not let that happen. But if it meant that Zeke's teeth weren't constantly chattering while we sat next to each other, if it meant that he stopped thinking that he'd actually seen a black van drive by, then I guessed it was okay. It let me keep doing what I needed to do. And it made him a little more excited about what we'd made together, that other people liked it.

Zeke and I sat in my car, the windows down, still baking, our sweat crystallizing, and I watched as he used all his different pencils, and he drew those hands, over and over. I loved watching the quick little movements, that singular moment when you realized what the lines were amounting to. And how, from that moment on, no matter what you did, no matter how you turned your head, you couldn't unsee it. For some reason, it was a magic trick that I never got tired of. As soon as he was finished, I'd ask him to do it again, and he'd simply flip to the next page in his sketchbook. It wasn't automatic, it wasn't rote. Each time, he thought about it, considered what he was doing, and I would sit and wait, trying to pinpoint the second that my eyes could see what I knew was coming. It was July. The summer wasn't going to last forever. Or maybe it would. I had no idea.

BRIAN TOLD US THAT HE SAW LYLE TAWWATER, WEARING AN Oakland Raiders T-shirt and black sweatpants, hanging up the poster on a gas pump at the Golden Gallon. Lyle was twenty-two and had broken his back in high school when his four-wheeler flipped. His sister had been riding behind him and was still in a coma at a hospital in Knoxville. And Lyle, this quiet little country kid, got real weird when he got out of the full-body cast, started going to flea markets and buying old fixed-blade knives and remaking them into strange, almost medieval-looking devices of violence, which he then sold at craft festivals. He always had the slightest fuzz on his upper lip, the most delicate blond hairs, but his eyes were crazy.

Brian asked Lyle if he was a fugitive, and Lyle smiled and put his index finger to his lips. He got back into his car and said, "I'm one of 'em," and drove off. Brian had removed the poster and showed it to me. It wasn't a Xerox of our poster, but Lyle's own version, the lines so dark and angry, almost vibrating. He'd re-created my phrase exactly, but the hands looked skeletal. And in the bed was a single person, a little girl, hooked up to machines.

I imagined Lyle, still living with his mom, sitting in his room and making more than a dozen copies of this poster by hand. It didn't make me sad for some reason. I mean, Lyle had always made me sad, to have ruined your life and the life of the person you loved most in the world because you took a turn too fast. But this felt like a kind of grace. I wondered how many he would have to hang for his sister to awaken from her coma. Whatever the number, however unlikely, it seemed worth trying.

And Zeke and I saw this girl, Madeline, hanging posters without any real fear of being caught, just stapling them to trees in the park. Madeline had been a cheerleader in junior high but then, I don't know exactly why because I wasn't aware of the complex negotiations required to be popular, she'd quit and started hanging out with the theater kids. She wasn't a goth, not really, because I don't think anyone really knew exactly what that was. I mean, she listened to Nine Inch Nails. She wore a lot of black eyeliner. We didn't know what to call that, but we just knew that Madeline was suddenly not the Madeline who had been the sturdy base of the pyramid during pep rallies. She was transformed.

I can't quite articulate how, in so many ways, Coalfield controlled how the outside world came to you. Like, you never really knew about punk until you heard Green Day on the radio, long after they were popular, and if you loved that, maybe you started doing a little work. I mean, we did not even have MTV in our cable package. You had to buy a *Spin* or *Rolling Stone*, and you started to work backward, learning about the Sex Pistols. And once you knew those two bands, you had to work harder to fill in the middle, and if you were lucky, somebody's cousin had given them a tape of Minor Threat and they gave you a dub of it. Or you went to Spinners and just looked endlessly at the used cassette tapes until you picked one that had an interesting cover, and maybe you just happened to buy Black Flag's *My War*. But, no matter what, you were never quite experiencing anything in a linear way. And you were always kind of embarrassed because you knew other people, people in Nashville or Atlanta (who could even conceive of New York City), knew all of this, in the exact order it was meant to be consumed, and so you didn't really talk about it. You kept it all locked up inside of you and suddenly you were sending cash in envelopes to record labels you read about in *MRR* and you got a 7" record of some punk band in Wisconsin that would never record another song.

It was like this for me with books. After I'd read every single Nancy Drew book twice, I found *The Chocolate War* in the school library, and I told the librarian that I liked it and so she gave me *The Outsiders*. And then my mom gave me Flannery O'Connor, and I started grabbing anything I could find and I had no idea what other people thought was good or what was important. And so I almost never told anyone what I liked because I was terrified that they would tell me how stupid it was. Every single thing that you loved became a source of both intense obsession and possible shame. Everything was a secret.

Madeline saw me staring at her, and she just smiled. I don't think she even knew who I was. But she made devil horns with her right hand and mouthed the words *We are fugitives*, and I nodded.

Zeke asked, "Who is that?"

I shook my head. "Just some dumb girl," I replied, and we drove to find a place that had a hidden spot that would accept what we'd made.

And we did find places. We did not stop. Zeke really got into taking empty two-liter Coke bottles and painting them gold and then making these lovely illustrations of wolves and flowers and intricate patterns with his fancy paint pens. We'd roll up one of the posters and slide it into the bottle and seal it up. Then we'd bury them around town, like time capsules. Each one we marked on the map with a little drawing of an hourglass. And each one was a different length of time. We'd open this one in five years. This one in ten. This one in twenty. Forty. Fifty. We were so young. It didn't seem that impossible to us, to jump on a plane, meet up in some run-down park with a single swing and a broken jungle gym, in our sixties, and dig up this time capsule, just so we could say, "We made that. It looks just like I remember." And then we'd bury it, leave it for someone else to find.

The cops were patrolling more frequently, but it still felt so unreal and they were looking for a black van, for hulking, greasy-haired roadies for Iron Maiden. And other teenagers, maybe even adults, had started doing it. The Kroger, which had a copier that was five cents a copy, no longer allowed people to use the machine, by request of the police. The library also had a copier, but they refused to keep their patrons from using it, although now this one librarian, Ms. Ward, who had the craziest dyed-black hair and must have been in her eighties, had to look at every document that someone wanted to copy. You could just drive thirty minutes to Manchester or some town that was big enough that you could go into a Kinko's and do whatever the hell you wanted. There was this little group of men, a very very sad militia, who would drink beer and then patrol the streets and tear down the posters and make a dinky little fire and sit around it and feel like they were protecting the town. And they were loud as hell, and they got winded walking too much, so then they'd jump into their trucks, and the police started assigning a patrol car just to make sure that they didn't shoot anyone, and so it was fairly easy to navigate all of this. And we mostly did it in the daytime, when no one cared, when no one saw us.

Zeke drew so much that he was already on his fifth notebook of the summer. The novel, somehow, had opened up. All I had to figure out was if my character would get away with it. I mean, of course she would get away with it, but I needed to figure out how spectacular the final crime would be. Zeke and I had only really known each other for a month and a half, but that initial little burst of physicality had burned off, and it made us more comfortable with each other. It wasn't weird to spend hours with just our knees touching. We never did anything else, like I never put my hand in his pants. He never touched my boob, and I think I would have died if he had. It was like we got the kissing out of the way, decided that was probably as good as it got before things got gross and weird and sad, and we just talked, nonstop, and enjoyed the fact that the other person was listening.

Zeke said that his mom had been talking to a lawyer in Memphis, a divorce lawyer, and she had mailed his mom a big envelope full of papers. Zeke's mom hadn't opened the envelope yet, but it was on the dresser in her room.

"So she's gonna leave him?" I asked Zeke.

He shrugged. "Maybe? I mean, if she signs the papers, I guess so."

"I'm sorry, and I know it sucks, but I'm kind of jealous of your mom. I wish my mom had been able to do that, to shove a big stack of papers right in my dad's face and be like *hit the bricks, motherfucker*. I think she'd be happier. We'd all be happier. He still would have left. He'd still have that other kid. But it would have been so sweet."

"I really don't want her to do it," Zeke admitted.

"I know. I mean, *I* want her to do it, but I know why you wouldn't."

"He hasn't called once," he said. "Or, no, I mean, I think he's calling, but he hasn't asked to talk to me."

"What an idiot. But, like, if your mom leaves him, will you guys stay here?"

"I don't know. My mom hasn't said anything about it. She doesn't say *anything*. She just plays music and stares at the wall."

"If you stayed, you'd be in school with me. Nothing would have to end, you know?"

"Yeah," he replied, but I could tell that it made him sad to think about it. I mean, who would want to go to school at Coalfield High?

"I don't really have friends," I finally said.

"I know," he replied. "You've told me. I mean, I have *some* friends."

We were quiet for a minute, and then he added, "Even if I go back to Memphis, we'll still be friends, right?"

"Yeah," I said. "I hope so."

A FEW DAYS LATER, LYLE TAWWATER DIED. HE FELL OFF THE water tower, where he had been climbing the ladder in order to put up posters at the top. Hobart told us about it, because he had been there when the police responded to a call from someone who found Lyle while they were walking their dog that morning. He said Lyle was folded up, broken, and there were about a dozen copies of the poster scattered around him. Hobart was as sad as I'd ever seen him. "That poor kid," he finally said.

"It's awful," my mom said, softening to him, holding his hand.

"If I hadn't written that stupid article," he said, but my mom shushed him. I could feel all these strange emotions swirling around inside of me, no way of expressing them in public, and so I went to my room. In the bottom of my sock drawer, I retrieved the poster that Lyle had made, the one my brother had taken. I loved it, truly. Lyle was dead. I was sixteen, you know? Everything about me was in constant flux, nothing had settled, and I felt so strange inside my body. But I was capable of guilt. Like Hobart, I wondered if I'd killed Lyle. I mean, I felt certain that I had, if you sat down and mapped it out. And every time I thought about it, that I was responsible for someone's death, I immediately pushed the thought away, tried to hide it under everything else that was inside of me.

I didn't really believe in a god, but I believed in penance, in reconciliation. And I knew what I needed to do was to stop hanging up my poster. And maybe that was why it hurt when I pushed Lyle out of my mind, because I wasn't going to stop, and it pretty much solidified the fact that I was a bad person. I was a bad person and I wasn't even trying to fight it.

I held the poster up to the light. Maybe my penance would be to make a hundred copies of it, to keep posting it, for Lyle, but I couldn't. It wasn't my poster. It didn't have any power over me.

I had to fold Lyle and his sister into our own poster, to put up twice as many. I wondered how many people could fit inside of our poster. Our poster. Me and Zeke. If I died, I really hoped Zeke would keep making them. If he died, I knew for a fact that I would. That's maybe what made me so sad about Lyle. His sister was in that hospital bed, far away from him; he had been alone when it happened. It was better, I decided, to have someone else.

IT ONLY GOT WORSE. THAT WEIRD DAD MILITIA, THE POSTER Posse, were constantly drunk, standing over the faint little fire that was burning on the sidewalk, and one of the men, Mr. Brewer, who worked in the sporting goods section of Wal-Mart, saw a black blur move quickly across the street, and he raised his shotgun and it went off, what they had taught us in the mandatory hunter safety course in eighth grade was an *accidental discharge*. He ended up shooting Mr. Henley, the auto shop teacher at the vocational school, right in the face. And though he didn't die, Mr. Henley spent the rest of the summer in the hospital and lost his right eye. Worse, two of the other men, one a deacon at the Presbyterian church, fired several rounds in the direction of where Mr. Brewer had shouted that he saw the dark figure. One of the bullets went through a window of the house across the street and grazed an elderly woman's neck. If the police hadn't already been on the scene, watching over the men to make sure they didn't burn down the whole block, she would have bled to death.

What Zeke and I couldn't figure out exactly, though we were still putting up posters with the same regularity, was how the whole town was continually papered over with what we had made. People were also just spray-painting bits of the incantation, or trying to re-create the hands, the paint dripping down, looking more like cow udders. I tried to consider which teenagers in Coalfield would be weird enough to do all this, what burnouts or druggies or goths or jokesters would be willing to perform such a feat, but I started to think that maybe it didn't matter who you were. Maybe it was just like any strange, zeitgeisty experience. You saw it was happening and either you resisted it (or blasted someone in the face with a shotgun) or you let it overtake you. And either way, whatever you did, it kept going, for as long as it wanted. And I hoped it would be forever.

We were eating corn dogs in my car, parked at the Sonic Drive-In, where the carhops wore roller skates and brought the food to your car on trays. Brian, who was a fry cook there, said the hot dogs were good because they fried them twice. Zeke paid for all of it. I was running lower than usual on funds because I hadn't been taking as many babysitting jobs, but Zeke simply told his mom how much he wanted that day, and she would produce the money without question.

"Are you guys rich?" I asked him. I knew he went to private school, but that only spoke of a wealth that was beyond me. He considered the question.

"I mean, I think so? Yes. I, like, wasn't sure when I was in Memphis, but now that I'm here this summer, in Coalfield? You know, looking around? I'm pretty sure we're rich."

Zeke was the kind of rich that I could tolerate, someone who didn't seem to know what that money could do for him. Maybe at a private school in Memphis, your mom a violin prodigy, the levels of wealth and privilege were such that it wasn't as helpful as I'd hoped. All that mattered to me, besides the fact that he could buy me four corn dogs if I asked, was that if things really got bad, if we got caught, his money might get us out of a jam.

As we drank our Ocean Waters, these horrible and wonderful blue coconut sodas served in an insulated cup so huge that if you drank all of it at once, you would fall into a coma from the sugar, Zeke and I talked about what we always talked about, trying to remember little bits of our past, trying to adequately explain ourselves to another person. I told him about my stocking that we hung up at Christmas, how the triplets' had little nutcrackers on them, blue and red and green, but mine was this angel who looked dead, its eyes closed and hands folded over its heart. Zeke told me about a mouse that he'd found in the backyard when he was six, injured by a stray cat, and how he'd kept it in his room and tried to feed it, until his mom found it dead under his pillow the next day. It was like, we had covered the big narratives, the ways our families had fallen apart, how we felt so different from everyone else, how desperately we wanted to make something important, and what was left was the actual stuff that mattered, that one night I'd had a nightmare and stumbled into the triplets' room and asked all three of them to let me sleep with them until Charlie, finally, let me crawl into his little twin bed. How in the morning, Andrew and Brian made fun of Charlie, and how he had slammed their heads together like Moe in the Three Stooges, and how I felt charmed by this, the first time my brothers' violence felt sweet to me.

And once we'd exhausted those stories for the present moment, wanting to space them out, hold on to them, we talked about the posters. "I was thinking about this last night," Zeke said. "Like, even if we stopped at this point, what would it matter?"

"It would matter a ton," I said, "to me."

"No, I know. I know that," he replied. He shook his head, trying to figure out what he meant. "I mean, what would it matter to the rest of the world? Other people are already doing it. Like, it will either keep going or stop no matter what we do."

"Well, okay, maybe."

"No, I think it's good, right? Like, we can keep doing it, and it's okay if we keep doing it, and even if bad stuff happens, it's not like we could stop it now."

"That's kind of philosophical," I said.

"Maybe," he admitted.

"I don't know anything about philosophy," I told him, "so I don't know if it's sound reasoning or not."

"Maybe I'm just trying to make myself feel better because that guy died," he said. And I knew this was coming. The first time I'd seen him after the news about Lyle came out, he had emphatically stated that he *did not want to talk about it*. And, selfishly, I had hoped maybe we would never have to talk about it.

"Oh, Zeke," I whispered.

He was quiet for a second. He took another bite of his corn dog. "We killed that guy, Frankie. I mean, we were a part of it, for sure. I don't care what you say, I know it's true."

"Well, yeah, we played a part in it. If we didn't exist, Lyle would probably still be alive."

"No, it doesn't have to be if we didn't exist, Frankie. You know, right? The big thing was that we made the poster. If we hadn't made the poster, he would still be alive."

"Yes," I admitted. "I know. But, it's not just us. If his sister hadn't gotten hurt. If she'd recovered. If those idiots hadn't lied about being abducted by Satan worshippers. If the news hadn't talked about it."

"I know. I don't think we have to take *all* the blame. But we have to take some of it. We really do."

"I'll take it," I said. "But that's as far as I can go with it. I'll accept it, but I can't change it."

Zeke looked at me and then nodded. "I think I'm just trying to figure out how I could have made this thing and still be a good person. Like, my intentions were good, right?"

"Yes, of course," I told him.

"And what we made was good," he said, and he sounded a little more confident now.

"It is good," I said. "It's the best thing ever."

"And so it just keeps going," he said. "Because it'll keep going with or without us."

I knew he was doing this for himself, that he wanted to know that he wasn't a bad person. And it made me love him, even as it made me feel a little bit worse about myself. Because I didn't care if I was a bad person anymore. I just . . . I just didn't.

AND IT SPREAD. IT'S HARD TO EXPLAIN TO ANYONE WHO DIDN'T grow up in the time before the internet how impossible this actually was, and for it to even reach me at that time meant that it was probably five times as prevalent as what I was hearing on the news or reading in the papers. This was not like a few years after that summer, when the whole chain of events was featured on *Unsolved Mysteries* and *Hard Copy* and *20/20* and before it was mentioned on *Saturday Night Live*, where it turned out that Harrison Ford was putting up the posters, though he blamed it on a one-armed man, and before the TV movie *The Edge: The Story of the Coalfield Panic* or the twenty-seven-song concept album by the Flaming Lips called *Gold-Seekers in the Shantytown*. This was before the streetwear company X-Large did an entire clothing line featuring the poster. This was before the Japanese streetwear company A Bathing Ape did a nearly identical clothing line featuring the poster five years later. This was before the series of articles in the *New York Times* about the Coalfield Panic won a Pulitzer Prize. This was before seven different people came forward to claim responsibility for the poster, before all seven of them were summarily disproven. This was before the poster had its own Wikipedia page, before there was theedgeisashantytown.com and wearefugitives.com and thelawisskinnywithhungerforus.com, which were the names of three different emo bands in the 2000s. This was before a wrestling message board said that the phrase came from a promo by the Ultimate Warrior that had never been released, and before people spent years trying to find a tape of it. This was before Urban Outfitters sold a print of the poster for forty-five dollars. This was before a famous chef in New York opened a fried chicken restaurant called Skinny with Hunger, which lasted less than a year. And before a huge contingent of citizens in a tiny Eastern European country overthrew their corrupt government, shouting, in English, "We are fugitives" as they stormed the president's mansion, and one of the rebels, a young woman who was honestly way too pretty to be dealing with corrupt governments, held up a sign that said the same phrase for an iconic photograph that was featured on the cover of *Newsweek*. It was before all of that, which was much harder for me to understand than anything that happened during that summer, even though I do not understand very much about that summer, because it still feels like a dream. Because my life still feels like a dream. Because every single time that I reassure myself that what I have, the life that I've made, is real, I find myself automatically going back to that summer and playing it over and over and over again in my mind, and I still can't quite tell you for sure that any of it really happened.

The only evidence is that I'm still here. And the poster is still here. And I know because I still have the original poster, with my blood and Zeke's blood on it. And if I start to lose a sense of myself, if I start to drift outside my life, I take the original poster and I make a copy on the scanner/copier/printer in my own private office, and I go somewhere, anywhere in the entire world, and I hang it up. And I know, in that moment, that my life is real, because there's a line from this moment all the way back to that summer, when I was sixteen, when the whole world opened up and I walked through it.

Ten

COALFIELD WAS NOTHING. THERE WAS NOTHING TO IT. IT WAS rural in the way that a lot of rural places existed in the mid-nineties, which is to say that it had a Wal-Mart and fast food and little subdivisions of houses of various levels of wealth and then fields and fields of soybeans. You would not come here unless you were visiting family or you got a job working at the Toyota factory or the air force engineering base a few towns over. What we had, everyone else had, too, and who wanted that? So it was such a strange sensation when Coalfield, because of us and whatever we'd done, became a place that mattered.

People made it a priority that summer to visit Coalfield. College kids, so handsome and tan, always a little drunk or high, showed up from Georgia and North Carolina, emptied out of cars, and just, like, walked around our town. They looked for the posters, and when they saw one, they stole it or took a picture of it. The Royal Inn, which was usually just for construction workers and weird sex stuff, was now completely full at all times, parties around the pool that the management hadn't even bothered to fill. Old hippies in RVs showed up with coolers filled with soggy sandwiches and orange soda, and they would set up a picnic in the state park and watch everyone else either put up or pull down posters. There were teenagers from all the surrounding counties, wearing T-shirts by bands like Napalm Death and Marilyn Manson and Soundgarden and Korn, and they had our poster in their hands, and they searched for a place to hang it.

Bethy Posey, who was crazy pregnant, which I could not imagine in this heat, and who was the same age as me but tiny like a doll, though now with a giant belly, had set up a table where she sold Xeroxes of the original poster. A dollar a copy. She had these customized versions with the word *fugitives* whited out and you could write your own name in the blank space and hang it up and take a picture of it. Her ex-boyfriend, Danny Hausen, who was training to be a professional wrestler, had done some posters where instead of the beds with the children, he had drawn Bart Simpson or Elmo or the UT Vols symbol.

It was a little like Lollapalooza, this kind of all-day event, but underneath that was this humming sensation, people waiting for something to happen. And so, of course, something occasionally did. Someone set fire to a tree in the square and it burned to nothing before the fire department even got there. Someone saw a black van parked at the Bi-Lo and this whole crew of townspeople beat the absolute shit out of it with baseball bats and hammers, and the cops had to show up to get everyone to disperse. At the public pool, a man kept throwing these fake gold coins at people and talking about how gold seekers were minions of the devil, and Latrell Dunwood tried to drown the guy, and it took six terrified lifeguards to stop him. The Poster Posse crouched in the bed of a jacked-up truck and drove all through the town, threatening to murder anyone who looked even the slightest bit like a fugitive or a gold seeker. The Presbyterian church's sign read IS GOD SKINNY WITH HUNGER FOR YOU? and Zeke said, "Shouldn't it say, *Are you skinny with hunger for God?*" and I was like, "Zeke, please."

It was absurd.

It's impossible to overstate how bizarre it was. There are now so many home videos on the internet of that summer, people just aimlessly wandering around, screaming out the phrase that I wrote. Discarded posters were constantly fluttering in the wind, blowing down the streets because people didn't really care if they stayed up.

It was also thrilling.

Zeke and I would drive all over town. I was spending all my money on gas. And every single poster that I saw, I didn't even have to think about it. It became a reflex. I just knew. They were mine. Or mine and Zeke's. What was the difference?

It was also frustrating as hell because it had been our thing, and no one else understood that.

They thought it was everyone's thing, and that made me want to drown someone in the public pool or set them on fire. I had wanted people to care, to notice, but I hadn't wanted them to put their own hands all over it, to try to claim it. But how do you stop something like that? You just tried to make more of it so you didn't lose your claim to what was inside of you.

Hobart said that the mayor, who was also the morning DJ at WCDT who handled the segment called, I am not joking, Rough Trade, where people called in to barter goods and services, had asked for the National Guard to come to Coalfield to maintain order, but nothing was happening yet because it wasn't really violent, or not violent in the way that would be improved by having a nineteen-year-old in camouflage trying to corner some other nineteen-year-old in a Blind Skateboards T-shirt. The cops had pretty much given up. I cannot imagine how many people they charged with vandalism in the first few days, but eventually the amount of work required to deal with it overwhelmed our dinky little police force. My brothers told me that some cops were just making people give them fifty dollars so they wouldn't get arrested, and they must have made at least a few thousand dollars doing this. All the restaurants were full. Kids sold Kool-Aid in paper cups and Little Debbie snack cakes from wagons that they pulled up and down the sidewalks. Action Graphix, which mostly sold trophies for Little League and signs for new businesses, had made a bunch of T-shirts with our poster on it and sold them from a van, a white minivan, that they drove around town. People were making money. Not me and Zeke, but other people. It was, I guess, good for Coalfield, but the people who lived here, who had never left and had no intention of ever leaving, began to feel trapped, afraid to leave their houses. So many people in Coalfield had guns, knives, fucking compound bows. They liked to show them off even when nothing was at stake. It seemed inevitable that someone was going to get hurt in a spectacular way, and I could feel the weight of that, but it wasn't like I could stop anything. If I admitted what we'd done, what would change? Would anyone even believe us?

My brothers were strangely unaffected by the panic. And, truly, my brothers lived for chaos, for anything that let them break or bend or stretch the world around them. They were just bored, or maybe it was more that they were mystified by the poster and it made their heads hurt. They tried to have sex with the college girls who showed up, and I think they probably did. They smoked weed and drank handles of George Dickel and watched the proceedings from afar. They did not even seem to remember that they had stolen a copier a year before, had no desire to participate. It was all beyond them. And I can't tell you how much this pleased my mother. Whatever was going on in Coalfield, her family was not responsible. The triplets had not done anything, and she dared the authorities to try and accuse them. Of course, she knew that I was weird, and she knew that Zeke and I were driving around all the time when we weren't hiding in my room, but she never seemed to consider that I had made this thing. She thought I was having sex. She thought I was *in love*. Under any other circumstances, I would have been so irritated by this, but since people in the fucking Rotary club were now destroying black vans with baseball bats to get at the Satan worshippers inside, I was slightly relieved that I wasn't suspected.

Zeke's mom, on the other hand, had barricaded herself in her childhood room, leaving Zeke to watch *The Price Is Right* with his grandmother, who wildly overestimated the price of everything, in the mornings, and then, after he'd hung out with me all day, he'd watch taped episodes of her favorite show, *American Gladiators*, with her, both of them uncomfortably marveling at the physiques of the gladiators. "Turbo looks a little like your grandfather as a young man," she once told him. "Of course, no one wore clothes like the gladiators in those days."

There was this unspoken rule in our relationship that I did not ever go over to his grandmother's house. I think it was that he was slightly embarrassed of his mom's catatonic grief and his grandmother's oblivious passivity, and he much preferred the jumbled, messy nature of my own family, where you could be weird and no one was going to make you feel bad about it, or at least they wouldn't hold on to it for long. He was always kind of wide-eyed around my brothers and my mom, like he didn't know families could be like this, and I think he liked that close proximity. Like, if an angry mob came for us, better to be here, where my brothers would at least seriously fuck up some people before they dragged us out of the house. Plus, his mom and grandmother never left the house, and my mom and brothers were almost never around during the day, so it just made more sense to hide in my room and talk about secret fantasies we had for the future.

In my room, both of us propped up in bed, on top of the covers, the fan blowing air that was just slightly cooler than the air outside right into our faces, it felt like we could ignore what was happening in Coalfield just long enough to not feel crazy. I was writing a little story to go along with this drawing that Zeke had done of a black van that had this sludgy purple liquid spilling out of the open side door. The story was about a guy, a bizarro Timothy McVeigh, who crammed vans full of dark magic, incantations, and left them in front of TV stations to unsettle the airwaves. And Zeke was drawing the cover to the novel that I was trying to finish, hoping that the professional font and the image of my evil Nancy Drew would spur me to the end of the story.

So much of my happiness of that summer was the smell of Zeke, kind of sweaty and a little like mothballs, and the sound of his pencils and pens scraping so softly against the paper. There were times when he didn't even feel real, exactly, like his body wasn't tangible to me, but there were these smells and sounds that reassured me that he was near, and I believed in them so much more than in his skin and bones, wrapped up in extra-large T-shirts and ragged, stone-washed jeans. I don't know if that's love, to need the sensations produced by the body more than the body itself. Not the kiss, but the taste of celery that came after. Not his hands, but the sound of his hands making art. Not the fact that he was here for only this summer, but the fact that I might find reminders of him in surprising places for the rest of my life.

And yes, that is lovely, and yes, I was a very repressed and strange girl who had never really connected with another human being, so I'm probably being overly poetic, because I also distinctly remember moments when I thought, *I'm going to die in Coalfield. The summer will never end, and I will never leave, and no matter how many posters we hang up, I'll never get out of here.* And there were times when I thought, *Zeke, goddammit, get me the fuck out of here*, but I was so scared that when he left, he would forget me. All he knew was me in Coalfield. So we had to leave, just for a second, I thought. There were so few spots on our map of Coalfield that weren't blasted with stars, the strangest constellations, and now that other people were doing it, too, maybe if we drove just a few hours in any direction, we'd find a spot that was pristine, that did not know about the edge, was so unprepared for it that we'd transform that new place before it had time to resist.

"We could go to Memphis," he offered. "I could show you around."

"Just you and me?" I asked. That felt like the most relationshippy thing in our brief time together, though I am now remembering that we did a weird blood pact and, you know, we were responsible for one of the weirdest mysteries in American pop culture. But that was all so strange, even the kissing, so outside of, like, corsages and airbrushed T-shirts with your names on them. This felt like the most normal thing a couple could do, spend a day in the city, and it was somehow more terrifying to me than blood. "We can put up the posters all over Memphis," I said, just to bring things back into a world that I understood.

"Yeah, that would be fun. We could go by my school and hang them up," Zeke said, and now I could see him starting to vibrate a little with the possibilities. "We can go to the zoo! We can get a Huey Burger. Maybe we could see a Memphis Chicks game. Have you ever been to Graceland?"

"You want to put up posters in Graceland?" I asked. I thought that if there was one place in the entire world where devotees would kill you for desecrating the sanctity of a holy space, it would be the mansion where Elvis played racquetball.

"No! Well, maybe. That would be pretty cool. I just mean, we can do the posters, absolutely, but I can also just show you around and we can do some fun stuff."

"Okay, yeah . . . I'm good with that. Rad."

"The thing is . . . ," he said, frowning.

"Yeah?"

"My mom would kill herself if she knew I was going to Memphis," he finally said.

"Do you have to tell her?" I asked.

"Are you going to tell your mom?"

"I am definitely going to tell my mom," I said. Aside from what I'd done this summer, I was a very good girl. I never wanted my mom to worry about me. She had been screwed over, so why would I make it worse for her?

"Well, I think I won't tell her, and as long as we don't die on the drive to Memphis, it should be okay."

"How many posters should we bring?" I asked.

"Fifty?" he said, but I could tell he was thinking about that Huey Burger or whatever the hell it was called. He wanted to show off how cool Memphis already was, not bring what we'd made in Coalfield to it. But do you think I cared about that?

"Let's bring a hundred," I replied. "Just to be safe."

I ASKED MY MOM THAT EVENING, AFTER THE BOYS HAD GONE out to meet up with friends. I'd made some brownies from a mix, because I knew she liked sweets, and we were watching Jackson Browne on *VH1 Storytellers*, a singer she loved so much, she had taped it earlier in the summer and would watch it while she drank a beer at the end of the day. Right after "Doctor My Eyes," her favorite song, I asked her if I could go with Zeke to Memphis.

"What now?" she asked, still humming the last song, but then she snapped to attention. I could tell she was a little irritated that I had messed up her moment of peace after a long day. She put her can of beer down on the coffee table and turned so she was facing me. "Memphis?" she repeated.

"Yeah, it's not really that far. Zeke wants to show me the city. Like, you know, the zoo? They have a zoo. Or . . . Graceland?"

"You want to drive all day to go see Graceland?" she asked.

"Well, not Graceland exactly. Like, not a specific place. Maybe we'll see a Memphis Chicks game."

"None of the things you've mentioned are things I've ever heard you say you like," she said. "Honey, I've been to Graceland. It's, you know, smaller than you think. It's really garish, but it's not worth driving that far to see it. I mean . . . he's no Jackson Browne."

"Okay, Mom, it's not what we'll do. It's just going somewhere. We haven't done any kind of summer vacation, like no beach or Disney World—"

"Now you want to go to Disney World? Honey, you would hate it, the crowds. You know your dad took me there for our honeymoon? Our honeymoon? The Magic Kingdom? My god, I should have known."

I realized that maybe the nearly empty beer on the coffee table had not been my mom's first one. She had mentioned the honeymoon at Disney World a dozen times since my dad had left us.

"It's not important what we do," I said. "I just want to get out of Coalfield for a day and have fun with Zeke. He wants me to see where he lived."

"Oh, honey," she said, smiling. "This is all very sweet. But that's so far. Why don't you just go to Chattanooga and see the aquarium. You love the fish there."

"Mom? Zeke wants me to go with him. He's excited. His dad has ruined his life, you know?" Was this too obvious, to talk about men who had messed things up for everyone else, all the good people left behind?

"You like him, don't you?" she asked. "Zeke?"

"I mean, he's my friend," I stuttered.

"Okay," she said, touching my face, like she was remembering something, but I didn't know if I was involved in the memory at all. "You're growing up so fast."

"It doesn't feel like that fast to me," I replied.

"It goes slow and fast at the same time," she told me. She looked so beautiful, my mom. I hadn't gotten what she had, the genes necessary to be that pretty, but I knew that I came from her. It made me so happy. This was maybe the moment when I could have told her that I'd made the poster, but why would I ruin this?

"You have to call me every few hours? Find a pay phone and let me know you're okay."

"I can go?" I asked.

"Yeah, sure," she said. I hugged her, and she laughed. "Okay, now let me eat these brownies and watch my man sing."

The next song was "Rosie" and I listened as Jackson Browne explained to the audience that it was about a guy he knew, the sound mixer, and how this girl in a green leotard had sat with him for the show and then left him for the drummer. It made me sad. It went on that the guy got drunk and tried to accost the drummer, and, right before the story ended and Jackson Browne started the song, he said that the girl had been sixteen.

"Sixteen?" I said, "Jesus, Mom."

"Don't mess this up," she said, waving her hand at me.

And then I listened to the song, which was so beautiful, so sad. And it hit me. I'd heard the song so many times, but who listens to Jackson Browne that closely? Like, what teenager in the nineties is reading the liner notes of a Jackson Browne album? When he sings that "it's you and me again tonight, Rosie," I realized he was singing about masturbating.

"Mom?" I said, just as the song ended. "Is he?"

"Is he what?" she said, shaking her beer can, making sure there was a little left.

"Is he talking about, you know, touching himself?"

"What? Ha, my god. Your mind. No, honey, I don't think so. I mean, this is *Storytellers*, right? He would have mentioned that. This is his chance."

"He is, I think," I said.

"He's not. Not to me."

"And that girl was sixteen. The one in the leotard. That's creepy."

"Well, it was the seventies."

"It wasn't creepy back then?"

"Well . . . no, it was. Honey, I love that song. I'm letting you go to Memphis. Don't make me regret that."

"Okay, okay, sorry," I said.

"Here's the thing, sweetie. If you love something, you can't think too much about what went into making it or the circumstances around it. You just have to, I don't know, love the thing as it is. And then it's just for you, right?"

"That's really philosophical," I offered. I don't know why I said this all the time, that things that were just slightly confusing were *philosophical*. Also, I want to say that in college or in grad school, I never took a single philosophy class. But I still say this sometimes when I get anxious about a thing I don't understand.

"Well, your mom is pretty smart," she told me, smiling. "Now please shut up. This next song is about a guy he knew who got killed trying to rob a place, and I swear to god, if you try to mess this up for me—"

"Okay," I told her. I kissed her cheek. "Thank you, Mom."

"You're welcome, sweetie," she said, and she let her mind settle back into something that would make her happy.

AND SO WE LEFT FOR MEMPHIS THE VERY NEXT DAY, JUST ME and Zeke, the car loaded down with Mountain Dew and Golden Flake chips and three boxes of Sugar Babies. Zeke played a cassette tape of Three 6 Mafia, because they were from Memphis, and, honestly, when I heard those horror movie pianos, I was like, "Oh, this feels like our poster." And there was all this weird imagery and devil-worship stuff, which I didn't know rap cared about, but then they started saying some really explicit stuff about the female body, and both Zeke and I got real red, and I put in Guided by Voices, and we listened to Robert Pollard sing. And I thought, *Yes yes yes yes yes*. To be a teenager, it takes very little to think that someone else might actually know who you are, even as you spend all your time thinking that no one understands you. It's such a lovely feeling.

THE MIDDLE PART OF TENNESSEE IS SO FLAT, AND WE JUST DROVE and drove, and the sky was a perfect blue, and it felt really good to leave behind a place I'd known my entire life, even if it was just for a few hours. And in our backpacks, the edge was there, on that yellow-tinged paper, and that time in the car, when we were between two places, merely in transit, made me happy. Zeke told me about one of his teachers, a woman in her sixties who had a sculpture at the Museum of Modern Art in New York City, who would sit in a recliner and almost never moved and called up each student so they could show her their work. She would hold it up to the light, squint, and say, "Almost," or "Not quite," or "Good enough," and then send you back to your desk. He said it was terrible in terms of imparting knowledge, like actual technique or instruction, but he really loved the idea that you could work on something, put everything you had into it, and she was like a Magic 8 Ball, and you just waited to know what your fate would be.

And then we were in Memphis. It was kind of run-down, crazy potholes and a lot of litter, but Zeke was so happy. We immediately got a Huey Burger, and it was so good, even more because Zeke kept going, "Mmmm . . . Oh, I missed Huey's," like he'd been away in a war or something. There was this white wall absolutely blasted with graffiti, black Magic Markers, things like *Karen & Jim were here* 6/7/96 and *M-town, baby!* I got out one of our posters, but instead, I grabbed a marker and wrote the whole phrase, and then Zeke drew a rough little sketch of the hands. He hesitated and then wrote *Zeke and Frankie*, and he looked at me, smiling. "They paint over the wall all the time to start fresh. It'll be gone soon." I touched the wall, traced our names.

We wandered the zoo, looking at elephants and monkeys, but the animals looked dazed and drugged. We got some Dippin' Dots, those weird space-age ice cream pellets frozen with liquid nitrogen, and we sat on a bench in Cat Country, watching the tigers stroll around, stretching and staring into space. The stripes looked like liquid if you stared long enough, a kind of Magic Eye poster, and I thought about what would happen if I climbed into their enclosure, tried to touch it. I thought about the tiger dragging me around and around and around by my arm, blood everywhere, and I let the little dots of ice cream dissolve on my tongue.

And then I got out a poster and folded it into a triangle. Zeke did the same. We sat on the bench and folded up about twenty posters into little origami. And as we made our way out of the zoo, we left them everywhere, little land mines that wouldn't hurt anyone, just enough of a detonation to please us.

I ASKED ZEKE IF WE COULD HANG UP MORE POSTERS, AND HE guided us to Overton Park, and we walked through the grass until we reached the Overton Park Shell, this crazy amphitheater that was kind of run down but still beautiful in the way that movies in the forties thought the future would look like. We put up twenty posters as quickly as possible, but the shell was so big that it kind of swallowed up the images, the words. I wished we had brought a thousand of them. I think Zeke could tell I was disappointed. "It works better in Coalfield, you know," he said, "because it's such a little place." And he was right, but it made me sad. I thought about Elvis Presley standing on this stage, singing out the words I'd written, hearing his deep southern accent on the word *hunger*, and it sounded so good in my head, like I could almost really hear it. But it passed. And it was just me and Zeke, the park wide open, the sun burning my skin.

"We should probably head back to Coalfield," I said, and he looked disappointed for a second, but then he nodded. He touched my hand and said, "Thanks for doing this with me."

I nodded, embarrassed. I kissed him and he kissed me back. "You can come visit me all the time when I move back," he offered. "You know how to get here now." I hated that he was talking about the time after he left me, when the summer was over. The summer would end, sure, but why couldn't we pretend that it wouldn't? Why did everyone want things to move forward, and why did I want to be frozen in a block of ice?

"Well, I don't know where you live," I told him.

"Do you want to see it?" he asked.

"Yeah . . . I think so," I said.

"It's not that far. Come on," he said, and we walked back to the car. We drove to an area called Central Gardens, which was very rich and the houses were all old. Some of them looked like castles, lots of stone, and I instantly realized that, even though I had known that Zeke was rich, I hadn't quite contextualized what that might truly look like. I was suddenly scared to see his house, preferring to think of him on his grandmother's sofa, a kind of experience that I could at least understand.

"Here it is," he said, and I parked in front of a house that was, thank god, a little more modest than the ones around it. It was more like a cottage, but it still looked so expensive, this pristine, two-story house with stone pillars holding up the roof of the porch. The front door was a kind of wood that seemed like it was a hundred years old. The yard was expertly maintained, not a single bike or rickety lawn chair on the grass. There was a swing on the porch.

"This is where you lived?" I asked him, and he nodded.

"I live here," he said, and his eyes were glazed over.

"It's really nice," I offered, so embarrassed that he had spent all that time on the bed in my room that had sheets from a garage sale.

"It doesn't look any different," he said, more to himself, like he'd thought that, without his mom and him there, the house would collapse in on itself like a Transformer or something to account for their absence.

"This is a really nice house, Zeke," I said, like I wanted him so badly to say, "It *is* a really nice house, and I am rich. But I'd rather be with you instead," but he just kept staring at it. It was three in the afternoon, the sun finally starting to ease up, making it a little more comfortable to breathe. My A/C wasn't great, and the car was straining, but we just kept idling in front of his house.

"Give me a poster," he finally said. He was closer to the backpack, but I didn't want to make it weird, so I twisted around and retrieved one. He folded it in half and got out of the car and walked to the mailbox, putting the poster inside. He came back and sat in the car, his legs shaking a little.

"Do you want to leave?" I asked, but he said, "Give me another one."

I did, and he said, "Come with me? Please?" and we got out of the car. I grabbed the tape, and we walked onto his porch. He held the poster against the front door, and I tore off two strips of tape, and we affixed the poster to the door of his home. We stepped back to look at it, and he said, "Can you imagine my dad's face when he sees this?" but I didn't even know what his dad looked like. But I nodded. "Skinny with hunger for us," I said, and just then the door swung open and this woman was staring at us. She had a bathrobe on, baby blue, and she was not that much older than us.

"What the hell are you doing?" she yelled, but then she instantly stiffened when she saw Zeke. "Oh god," she said.

I said, "We're . . . collecting money for orphans. We're orphans," but she was already running out of the entryway.

"Zeke?" I said.

"We better go," he said, but he hesitated, thinking about taking the poster back, and then a man appeared, wearing only boxers and a T-shirt. "Son?" he said. The woman was peering out from another room.

"Dad?" Zeke said.

"What are you doing here?" his dad said. "Why didn't you call?" His eyes got a little wild, and he said, "Is your mother here? Did she send you?"

"It's just me," Zeke said. "And . . . this is my friend."

"Hello," I said.

"Why are you here?" his father said, now getting angry because he was no longer terrified that his wife was about to stab him.

"We went to the zoo," I offered.

"Who is this?" his father asked.

"I told you," Zeke said, starting to stutter.

"What is this?" his father asked, nothing but questions, this guy. Nothing about missing his son, no apologies, no explanation for why he was at home with some woman young enough to be his daughter in the middle of the fucking afternoon on a weekday. He grabbed the poster and examined it.

"This is . . . this is what they've been talking about on the news. This is everywhere."

"It's like . . . graffiti," Zeke offered.

His father's eyes widened and he looked at Zeke. He looked down at the poster and then back at his son. "You drew this," he said. It wasn't a question. He had moved on to declarative sentences. "You did this."

"We both did," I offered. "I wrote it," and he said, "Excuse me, miss, I am talking to my son right now."

"Well, okay, but—"

"Son, this is very bad. This is . . . this is really bad. You are going to ruin your life."

"Who is that lady?" Zeke suddenly asked. "'Cause that's not either one of the ladies that Mom told me about. Is she living here?"

"The fact that you are trying to turn this around on me," his father said, "to deflect blame for . . . this thing. Jesus Christ. Your mother has made you crazy."

"I hate you so much," Zeke said.

"Get in this house right now," his father said, almost yelling. "You want to go to jail for . . . this poster? I cannot believe—"

"I hate you," Zeke said again, rubbing his face with his hands, like he was trying to scrub dirt off, like there were bugs on him, like he was starting a fire inside of his brain.

"Get in the house," his father said, teeth gritted. "We need to figure out what we're going—" and Zeke suddenly leaped toward him and started scratching his father's face, digging his nails into the skin, and Zeke's father began to howl.

"Reuben!" the lady shouted.

"Shit!" his dad said, trying to tear his son's hands from his face, but Zeke was like a rabid squirrel. I ran forward and kicked his father as hard as I could, and his knee buckled and he was on the floor. It had nothing to do with my own dad. I just so badly wanted to hurt the person who had hurt Zeke. "Shit!" he shouted again.

"I'm calling the cops!" the lady yelled, but Zeke's dad shouted, "Sheila, are you crazy? Don't do that!"

"Come on," I said to Zeke, who finally pulled his hands from his father's face. There were these jagged little cuts all over his face, and I could see this flap of skin stuck on Zeke's fingernail.

We ran back to the car, and I burned rubber pulling away. We were both nearly hyperventilating, and I was going fifty-five miles per hour in a residential area, but I just kept going. I blew right through a stop sign and there was an old lady walking her dog who shouted at me, but I screamed, "Fuck off!" and kept going. Finally, after a few miles, I pulled into the empty parking lot of some auto parts store that had gone out of business.

"Oh, fuck," Zeke said, his whole body tensed like he was waiting for something to hit him. "We are so fucked."

"It's okay," I said. "You did the right thing."

"I just . . . Frankie, I'm so sad," he said, and he started sobbing.

"It's okay," I told him. He was shuddering, making these little screechy sounds as he tried to breathe. It scared me. "It'll be okay."

"My whole life," he said, but there was nothing else for a few seconds, just more sobs. "I wish I was dead."

"No," I said. "No, if you died, Zeke. If you died, I'd kill myself. Don't die. Okay? Don't die. You can keep living, okay? I'm alive, right? You think your life is worse than mine?"

"What do I do?" he asked, like I knew. Like he truly believed in me.

"Here, just . . . just come here," I said. I pulled him across the seat, and we awkwardly held on to each other. His face was so wet with tears and snot and drool and sweat. But he'd said he wished he was dead, so I held on to him. And then he kissed me, his mouth so salty. There was a little blood inside his mouth, maybe from biting his tongue while trying to murder his father, and I could taste that, too. I wanted to stop, to just listen to him breathe normally. If he could just regulate his breathing, I thought it would be okay, but he kept kissing me, rougher. He was pushing his tongue into my mouth, and I hated this instantly. I just kept thinking, *Don't die don't die don't die don't die don't die*. But was I talking to myself now? Or

Zeke? Both of us? It was hard to do anything else but let him kiss me and not die.

And then he started crawling onto my side of the car, pushing me against the door. And his hands started touching my body, and no one had ever touched my body. And I had wanted to keep it that way for as long as I could. I liked Zeke so much. But I didn't want him to put his hands in my pants in an empty parking lot in Memphis right after he'd yelled at his father because he'd been having sex with some lady in the afternoon. There is maybe no right time for someone to put their hands under your shirt, or there wasn't for me, but this was a really bad time.

"Zeke, please," I said, but he kept kissing me so hard, trying to take off my pants, and it was difficult for me to breathe, and he said, "I like you so much, Frankie. I like you so much." And I started to go deep inside of myself for a second, to make it quiet, and he said, "Do you want to do this? Could we do this?" and it was like I was sinking beneath the surface of a lake, not leaving my body but going deeper into it, and then I just . . . I don't know what I did. But I filled up my body again, my skin tightening around whatever it was that made me a human being, and I pushed Zeke away.

"Zeke," I said, "please don't. Okay? Please don't do that." And he seemed to kind of snap back to being that weird little boy I'd first met at the pool.

"I'm sorry," he said. He started crying again, which I could not handle. He could cry about the other thing, but not this.

"Zeke! Please. Okay? It's okay. You didn't do anything. You didn't hurt me. You stopped, okay? We're okay. You're okay."

"I'm so sorry," he said, but, like, who cared? It had happened and it hadn't quite happened, and I felt like I was safe now. I thought maybe it could go back to how it had been. I didn't know what else to say or do.

"The edge is a shantytown filled with gold seekers," I said, and Zeke said, "Oh, Frankie, I'm so sorry," and I said, "Shut up. The edge? The edge? It's a shantytown, okay? Just shut up for a second and breathe. The edge is a shantytown filled with gold seekers. We are fugitives, and the law is skinny with hunger for us."

"Okay," he said, "okay."

"We are fugitives, Zeke. We are fugitives. We are fugitives. We are fugitives, and the law is skinny with hunger for us."

"Okay," Zeke said, a kind of submission. "Okay, Frankie."

"No, just, let me do it. The edge is a shantytown filled with gold seekers," I kept going. I said it ten times. Twenty times? I don't remember. I didn't know how long we'd been there. I had to call my mom soon, find a pay phone to let her know that I was coming home. I was going back to Coalfield, and nothing had changed. As long as I kept saying the phrase, nothing would change. Zeke would not leave. He would not hurt me. He would not hurt himself. I said it again. And again. Zeke had stopped crying. I kept saying it, and he finally looked up at me, made eye contact. I kept saying it. Again and again, until he knew. Until he knew that I'd never stop saying it. For as long as we lived, I would never stop saying it. And we would live forever. So it would go on forever. It would never stop.

I said it again. And again. *The edge is a shantytown filled with gold seekers. We are fugitives, and the law is skinny with hunger for us.* I'm saying it right now. I've never stopped saying it.

Eleven

HOW ELSE COULD IT HAVE ENDED? I DROPPED OFF ZEKE, AND HE didn't even say goodbye. And when I got home, my brothers were in the living room and my mom was on the phone pacing in circles, asking, "How hurt are you?"

"What's . . . what's happening?" I asked.

"You didn't see when you drove home?" Andrew asked. When I shook my head, Brian told me that the Poster Posse had cornered a group of about five or six teenagers from our school, who were putting up more posters. The kids had painted their faces like Brandon Lee in *The Crow*, and when all the drunk old men in hunting orange threatened them, Casey Ratchet had thrown a bottle, knocking out Mr. Ferris, who ran the pool supply store out on the highway. And another man, they didn't know who yet, had shot Casey, point-blank in the chest. And Casey was dead.

"What now?" I said, stunned.

"Casey Ratchet fucking died, Frankie," Charlie said. "Hobart's on the phone with Mom, because it's bedlam over by the strip mall. It was all in the parking lot by Diamond Connection. He was there interviewing the Poster Posse. I guess somebody trampled him, and his leg is broken or something."

"Casey Ratchet?" I said again. Casey was maybe five feet, four inches, but he had been in *Thrasher Magazine* and was a sponsored skater. He'd spent spring break in California filming a skate video. He got suspended as a freshman for dyeing his hair pink and had been cited lots of times by the police for skating on private property. He had never said a single word to me, but I'd always thought he was cool, was destined to leave Coalfield and do neat things. And he was dead.

"If you told me that Casey Ratchet had made the poster," Andrew said, "I'd believe it. That would make sense. Remember, he had that Suicidal Tendencies T-shirt?"

"You think Casey made the poster?" I asked.

"I'm saying, I'd believe it if it turned out it was him," Andrew clarified.

"I don't know if anyone actually made it," Brian offered. "Like, I think the CIA started it as a kind of mind-control experiment. To see what would happen. That's why I never fucked around with it, because I didn't want to get disappeared by some secret government hit squad."

"I still think it's lyrics from a song," Charlie said. "Like, I know I've heard it before." Then he kind of did a faux–heavy metal screech. "Tha EDDDDGE is a shantytown . . . ," he said, sounding like Axl Rose.

My mom was off the phone and ran over to me. "You okay?" she asked. I nodded. "Hobart broke his leg, for crying out loud. I have to go get him from the emergency room and take him home." She looked at the triplets. "Don't leave this house," she told them. "Protect Frankie, okay?"

"Mom," I said, "I don't need them to protect me."

"I'll be back in a few hours," she said.

The triplets went outside to shoot baskets, and I stood in the living room, the house now empty. I wanted to tell Zeke what had happened. I felt like if he heard about it from anyone but me, he'd lose his mind. I was still holding my backpack. I opened it and there were four posters left, slightly crumpled. I went out the front door and just kept walking. It took about twenty minutes to walk the four blocks, but I could see the light on in his room. I went to the window, crouching in the bushes. I realized that I could very easily get shot, or reported to the police. I tapped on the window, standing on my tiptoes. And I saw Zeke's face through the glass, but he couldn't see me because of the glare. He was just staring out into the dark, his eyes so unfocused. He looked sadder than I'd ever seen him before. "It's me," I said, but he didn't open the window. He just stood there for a few more seconds and then walked away. I tapped again, but he didn't even come back. I took one of the posters out of my backpack and folded it a few times, made a square, and I wedged it in the little crack of the window where the window meets the frame, sliding it as far as I could into the slit, hoping he'd see it. I waited for five minutes, tapped two more times. Nothing. I didn't want to be gone when my mom got back home, so I finally gave up. I had three posters left, and I felt like God in the most ridiculous way, like no one in the world knew what I knew, not even Zeke. I picked three random mailboxes and slid the posters into them, pulling up the red flag on each one.

Back home, I crawled into bed, and I didn't wake up until a little before noon. The whole house was already empty, and I had no idea what else had happened the night before. I didn't leave the house. I waited and waited and waited for Zeke to show up, like always, but he never came. I went into the garage and spent the rest of the afternoon making more copies of the poster on the Xerox machine. I almost never handled the original copy, was afraid to damage it. But that day I used it to make the first copy, and then I stared at it, looking for anything that I might have missed before, tried to count every single droplet of blood, tried to determine which splotches were mine and which were Zeke's. I knew the world was going on outside, that things were happening, that large forces were now having to contend with this thing that I had started, but it felt so disconnected from reality.

When I was done making copies, I put my hand on the glass and made a single copy of my palm. I looked at the lines, wished I knew how to read them. I wanted to know what my future was, because in that moment, I could not imagine a future at all. I could not imagine how in the world I would keep this secret for the rest of my life. But I knew I would. And even then, sixteen years old, I knew that I would hate every person in my life who loved me, who took care of me, who helped me find a way to whatever life I would have, because I could never tell them who I was, what I'd done.

MAZZY BROWER

MAZZY CALLED AGAIN A FEW DAYS LATER, AND I ANSWERED IT.

"Okay," I told her.

"Okay?"

"I'll talk to you. I'll tell you."

"Wow . . . well, thank you, Frankie. This is a good thing, I promise. I'll do this in a way that honors your story."

"Okay," I told her. "I have to go."

"Wait, just . . . why did you say yes?"

"I don't know, honestly," I said. "Mostly I'm tired. I've been feeling a little crazy ever since you called. And I figured it would only get worse. Maybe I want to say it out loud and prove that I didn't make all of it up. I don't know. But something like that, I guess."

"When can I talk—" she started to ask, but I hung up the phone.

I was so close to the end. Not the end of the story, of course, because that would keep going, on a loop, forever. But I was getting close to the end of it being a secret. I wanted to go to bed, but it was ten in the morning. There were dishes to wash, a book that I wasn't writing, box tops I needed to cut out for Junie's school. But I went to bed. I got right back into bed, and I let myself dream about that summer.

Twelve

AT FOUR O'CLOCK, I COULDN'T STAND IT ANY LONGER, AND I drove over to Zeke's grandmother's house. I had filled my backpack with the posters, as if I couldn't function unless they were close to me. I knocked on the door, but no one answered. I pounded and pounded, yelling for Zeke, and then I went around the house and climbed the steps to the back porch. As I peered through the glass of the door, I saw him, crouched in the hallway.

"Zeke!" I said. "Can you talk?"

He shook his head, but I wouldn't leave. He had to know that I wouldn't leave. "Zeke! What the fuck?" I yelled, and then he finally came outside, closing the door quietly behind him.

"Are you, like, are you trying to hide from me?" I asked. "Is it because of what happened in Memphis? In the car?"

His face reddened, this crazy blush, and then he wouldn't look at me. "It's . . . I'm leaving. We're leaving." And his eyes got big for a second, like maybe he was scared I thought that he was including me, but I was still trying to figure out what was going on. "My mom and me . . . we're going back to Memphis."

"What? When?"

"Now. Well, tomorrow."

"You're leaving?"

"My dad called my mom last night," Zeke said. "He told her what's going on. He said I'm in danger of ruining my life. He says I could be arrested. He said I wouldn't get to go to college, and I was going to tell him that I'm going to go to art school, but—"

"Zeke, please. You're leaving? You're just going back? To your dad? That fucking asshole? Your mom is going back."

"She's scared, Frankie. I'm scared. It's scary. We could get arrested."

"We already knew that, right? We already knew that and it was . . . it was fine."

"They're worried about me. My mom says that Coalfield is not safe. Another kid died, Frankie. Like, Jesus Christ, this is really bad."

"Don't go," I said.

"I have to," he replied.

"Please don't leave," I said, grabbing his arm.

"Frankie, I don't have a choice, okay?" he said, and his voice cracked so hard, like puberty had just that moment kicked in for him. "I have to go home."

"Please stay here," I said. "Stay with your grandmother."

"God, no, I can't do that," he said. "This is bad, Frankie. It was good when it was just you and me. It was the best thing ever. But it's bad now. We did something awful."

"That's not true, and you don't even fucking believe that," I said, my voice rising. "You sound like you're reading a dumbass letter of apology to a judge."

"That kid died, Frankie. Like, we got him killed."

"No, no, no, no, no," I said. I did not want to rehash our responsibility as artists, did not want to keep explaining it away. I just wanted to be alive, to be in it, to keep doing it. And I needed Zeke. "I have all these posters. I have more of them back home. Let's hang them up. I think if we keep doing it, it'll keep going, and maybe it gets better. Maybe it turns into something else."

"I'm leaving," he said. "I'll write to you, though. Letters? I'll write when this is all over. And then . . . you know, you can come see me in Memphis."

And I knew right then that I'd never see Zeke again. This was the end of something that had mattered so much to me, for such an intensely short amount of time, and it was ending, and I was going to be all alone when whatever was next finally came for me.

He turned away from me and opened the door.

"I'll tell people we did it," I said. I opened my backpack and showed him the huge stack of the posters. "I'll put them all over this house and my house, and I'll tell everyone that it was us."

Zeke froze and then I watched his shoulders seize, like I'd just punched him in the neck. "No, you won't," he said. He was tapping the palms of his hands against his ears, like they were on fire, or maybe buzzing. He was right next to me now, and he suddenly grabbed my wrist, harder than I think he meant to. "Please don't do that," he said, and he wasn't even really looking at me, like he was far away. "I'm begging you not to do that."

I tried to pull my arm from his grip, but he squeezed tighter, like he couldn't let go until I promised him. The look on his face, it was like nothing I'd seen before from him. The left side was spasming, like bugs were under his skin, and he looked . . . so frightened. And I realized that he was afraid of me. Because I was doing something cruel, because I was terrified of being alone. Because I worried what I'd do if Zeke wasn't around, when it was just me and whatever was inside of me. Maybe, I thought, Zeke was what was keeping me from doing bad things.

I heard his grandmother call out from the kitchen, "Who's out there?" and Zeke pushed me away from him, as if he was trying to hide me from her. My feet were still firmly planted, and I stumbled backward. I dropped the backpack and then tripped over it, and then I was falling down the steps of the porch, one arm behind my back and the other reaching out for balance. I heard this snapping sound, felt this unbelievable wave of pain, so sharp that I gasped, but nothing came out of my mouth. My face hit the ground, my teeth biting into the dirt, and my mouth was instantly numb. After a second or two, I tried to stand because I was so embarrassed of myself, but I fell right back down. I must have had a concussion, had blacked out for a second, and I kept trying to understand why I couldn't get up, why I kept sprawling around in the grass behind Zeke's grandmother's house. And then I heard Zeke make this sound. It was so deep, a kind of retching moan, like a cow had been hit with a sledgehammer. And I was so afraid for Zeke. I tried to call out for him, but I still couldn't make a sound.

"Frankie," he said, "oh god, oh my god, oh god, oh my god." And he kept talking but it wasn't even real words, just sounds, little grunts, barks.

I finally rolled onto my back and sat up, and I realized that my left arm was snapped in half, just flopping around. It didn't hurt exactly, not like I expected—I guess I was beyond that kind of pain—but it also didn't feel like it was a part of my body. It was this thing that I didn't need, but I couldn't get rid of it. The backpack was still caught on one of my feet, a strap hooked around my ankle, and I used my good arm to get myself free. I took a deep breath and then stood up. I looked at Zeke, but he didn't come for me. That was worse than the broken arm, that he just stood there. He was crying, I could see that, but he wouldn't come any closer. There was a moment when he suddenly seemed to come back inside of himself, to realize what he'd done.

"I'm so sorry, Frankie," he said.

And I wanted to say that it wasn't his fault, that it was an accident, but maybe everything is an accident. Maybe nothing in the world is intentional. Maybe everything that has ever happened and ever will happen is some dumb mistake. So who cares if you apologize?

So I said, "Fuck you," and then I limped to my car, somehow getting into the driver's seat before I realized that I didn't know where the keys were. I used my good hand and my teeth to open the backpack, but only the posters were in there. I tried to use my left hand to reach into my pocket, but it didn't work, of course, and so I had to use my right hand and reach across into the left pocket of my jeans, and now the waves of pain, these intense shocks every time I shifted my body, started to hit me. But I got the keys, finally. It felt like it had taken four hours to do it.

I put the backpack on the passenger seat and started the car. I looked at the house, and Zeke was staring at me from the window of the living room. His grandmother was in the other window, so confused, frowning at me. I have no idea what she had seen or what she thought had happened or what her daughter had told her about Zeke and why they were returning to Memphis. And, like an idiot, I waved to her. Not to Zeke. I couldn't look at him anymore. But I waved to his grandmother, whom I had never spoken to in my life, and she waved back. And then I left.

It was such a short drive, but I was crying and panting, and the pain at this point was so intense that I felt like I was going to throw up at any second. I thought maybe I should drive to the emergency room. My mom wouldn't be home for at least an hour. This was all happening in a split second. My brain was misfiring, time had stopped, and I was looking into the future and the past at the same time. I imagined what I would say. I'd say, what, that I fell? And why couldn't I have said that? I could have said, *I fell down the stairs of my own house, not someone else's house, you understand, and that's how I broke my arm.* But for some reason, because my brain was shutting down in order to keep me from realizing how fucked up my body was, I thought I'd have to tell people that Zeke had pushed me. I had a bruise on my wrist from where he'd grabbed me. I thought he'd get in trouble. And so, what else could I do? Also, it felt like my life was ending, like the best part of it was gone forever, and maybe I wondered if it was worth it to keep living. I was curious how you made something end. I was in a car, and I was so close to my house. There wasn't much time.

There was this tiny little sliver of light, this one possibility, and it was all I could do to follow it, to walk into it. And so, just a few yards from my own house, I floored the accelerator of my car, the engine revving up so hard that it was screaming, and I drove right into the biggest tree that I could see, in our neighbor's yard. I crashed into it, this spectacular sound of metal just absolutely giving up its shape, and even though I had on my seat belt, which, honestly, I did not even remember putting on, my forehead hit the steering wheel and the world really did go black, the most perfect blackness that I have ever seen.

And when I woke up, I could hear the engine making such unnatural sounds, all this steam or smoke or something, maybe its soul, leaking out of it. The inside of the car was covered in posters, which had shot out of the backpack on impact, and I had double vision, and I was staring at the thing that Zeke and I had made, but I didn't remember that we'd made it. For those few seconds, I didn't know anything. I wasn't even sure that I was still alive. And then it came back to me, the whole summer, every single detail. And I thought, *I guess I'll die now.*

"Miss?" someone said. The formality of it was so shocking, so strange, like the maître d' of the fanciest restaurant in the world had just greeted me.

"Yes?" I answered, unsure of what exactly was happening.

"I'm going to help you, okay?" the voice said. "I've called for an ambulance, and they'll be here very soon. You're safe. Just stay awake. Talk to me."

I finally could see the man, and it was our neighbor, Mr. Avery. He was wearing that haori, and he looked beautiful, his hair so fine and blond.

"Oh, Mr. Avery," I said. "I'm so sorry about the tree."

"It's not my tree," he said. "It doesn't matter. I'm just so relieved that you aren't dead."

"It's my fault," I told him.

"It's no one's fault," he said, and he smiled, and he reached his hand toward my face, which was bleeding. He softly brushed the edge of his index finger back and forth along my left temple, and it is still the most comforting thing that I've ever felt in my life, that little point of contact, the softest touch, reminding me that I was not dead.

And then Mr. Avery looked inside the car and saw the posters. And he looked at me, and there must have been something in my eyes, because he knew instantly. He knew. I wasn't a copycat. His neighbor, that quiet, weird little girl, had made this poster.

He gave me a quizzical look, and I nodded. "It's me," I said.

"You made this," he said, a declaration.

"I made it, and I hung them up, and I'm still hanging them up." It was such a strange sensation, to admit this. I'd thought I would go my whole life not telling anyone. I'd told so easily. Well, I mean, I had almost died and the boy I loved had broken my arm, but still. I had been dying to tell someone, I now realized.

"That's . . . that's absolutely lovely."

"Really?" I asked.

"This is so strange, but please tell me your name again. I don't know if I've ever heard it."

"Frankie," I said.

"Oh, lovely. Frankie, you are the first person in this town who has surprised me. In the span of about two minutes, you have done the two most surprising things I have ever seen in Coalfield."

What a strange thing to say to a teenager who had almost died, either by accident or on purpose, but it filled me with such gratitude.

"My mom," I sputtered. "The ambulance . . . I can't let anyone find these."

"Oh, no. Okay, I see what you mean."

"My arm is broken," I said.

"It is, very badly," he admitted. He reached through the window and picked up a few of the posters that were near me. Then he went around to the passenger side and collected all of them. He was stuffing them into the backpack, and I could hear the ambulance.

"They're really close," I said.

"I've got them, almost," he called out. "Okay, I've got them—oh, there's one more under the seat. Okay, I have them all."

"Can you keep them for me? Hide them?"

"Oh, yes, that's exactly what I'll do. I'll hide them. It's our secret. It's—oh god, tell me your name one more time."

"Frankie," I said. The ambulance was so close.

"Frankie, I will never tell a single soul. Do not worry."

"Thank you," I said.

"Don't die, Frankie," he said. "If you died, I think I'd have to tell someone."

"I'm not going to," I said, and I must have sounded disappointed.

"You are going to have such an amazing life, Frankie," he told me. "If this is how it starts? It's almost breathtaking how good your life will be."

"I think I'm a bad person," I said.

"No," he said, and I thought he might say more, but then the paramedics were running up to my car, shouting things, and Mr. Avery vanished from sight. And I never spoke to him again. But sometimes, when I think, for the millionth time, that I'm a bad person, I can still hear his voice, that single word, *No*, and even if I don't entirely believe him, it's saved me so many times.

I WOKE UP IN THE HOSPITAL, MY OWN ROOM, AND EVERYTHING was numb and fuzzy. My whole body felt like it had this very very low level of electricity moving through it. My tongue felt huge inside my mouth, which also felt huge, somehow. My arm, the broken one, was held up by a rope or something and there was a splint made of foam and metal holding it in place. I was just starting to realize that it was still connected to my body when I heard my mom ask, "Frankie?"

"Yeah?" I said.

"You're okay," she told me. "Your arm is going to be fine, you know, brand new, at least that's what the doctor said. It was a fracture but, you know, the bone didn't—" My mom stopped suddenly and looked like she might throw up. I realized, now that the world was regaining a little clarity, how pale she looked. After a few seconds, she went on like I hadn't just seen her almost vomit over the horror of my broken arm. "It didn't break the skin, right? And teenage bones are, like, my god, they just go right back together and it's like nothing happened."

"My mouth feels funny," I told her.

"Yeah, you chipped your front teeth. We'll need to have a dentist fix your teeth, because they're . . . well, don't worry about your teeth, Frankie, Jesus. I'm not going to worry about your teeth, okay? The teeth are the *least* of our worries. But, yes, you messed them up pretty bad in the wreck."

"In the wreck," I said, like I was piecing together what she knew and what she didn't know. I wondered if Zeke had come to check on me, if he was in the hallway.

"Do you remember the wreck, sweetie?" she asked. "You drove right off the road. You drove . . . well, you drove a decent way into the neighbor's yard and hit their tree. Do you remember that?"

"I do," I admitted. "I hit their tree pretty hard."

"You absolutely did, sweetie," my mom said. "And, I just . . . Frankie, what happened?"

I knew I had to lie, and I knew it would be so easy to lie. The only problem was if Zeke was in the hallway, if he had told her everything. But I felt like he wasn't there. He had left me on the ground in his grandmother's yard. He hadn't come to help me. He was gone.

"Zeke's gone," I said.

"What now?" she asked.

"Zeke's leaving. Mom, is Zeke here? Like, is he here right now?"

"Do you think that Zeke is in the room, Frankie?" she asked, confused.

"No, but . . . is he in the hallway? Like, have you seen him?"

"Frankie? No. No, I haven't seen Zeke. I was at work and then I got a call from the police that you were in a car accident and it was really bad—well, it turned out it wasn't bad, okay? You're fine, and you'll be fine—and I drove straight here to the hospital, and I've been with you ever since."

"Okay . . . well, Zeke is going back to Memphis. He's leaving Coalfield." I started to cry.

"Sweetie, oh god. I'm so sorry. I'm so sorry because I know you really liked him," she said, patting my head, afraid to hold me because of how much pain I could theoretically be in.

"I miss him already," I said.

"And, honey, you were upset after he told you?" she asked me. "And you drove home?"

"Yeah . . . and I guess I was driving too fast, or I just wasn't concentrating on the road, maybe? I don't really remember, Mom."

"Well, okay, that's . . . of course you might not remember. But . . . Frankie? Can you look at me, sweetie?"

"I am looking at you," I replied.

"You're kind of looking about six or seven inches to the left of me, but that's . . . okay, maybe we'll ask the doctor about that when he comes back to check on you. But I just want to be sure of something. And you can tell me. You can tell me anything."

"Okay," I said, knowing that I wouldn't tell her everything. I would leave so much out.

"You didn't drive into the tree on purpose? Because you were upset that Zeke was leaving?"

"No!" I replied, because it really wasn't true. It was more complicated than that, but I wasn't getting into it. "Mom, no. I just . . . I don't know. I didn't try to kill myself, Mom."

"Oh, sweetie, just hearing you say it makes me feel a little sick," she told me. "And Zeke seems like a sweet boy, but, god, Frankie, don't ever kill yourself over a boy. Or anything! There's nothing worth killing yourself over. Your dad left me and started a whole new family. But I wouldn't kill myself over that."

"Mom," I said, suddenly so tired, "I don't want to talk about Dad right now."

"Of course not, sweetie," she said. She started to choke up, her eyes welling with tears. "I just . . . you are the most beautiful and wonderful and strangest person I have ever met. You are the most amazing person in the world. And you just have to live long enough to make the rest of the world understand that, okay? You have to stay alive."

"I'll try, Mom," I said, and I started crying again.

"In ten years," she said, "when you're out of Coalfield and you're successful and happy, you won't even remember this summer, sweetie."

"I think I will," I told her.

"Well, you'll remember it," she said, "but it won't be as important as it seems right now."

—

THINGS MOVED QUICKLY AFTER THAT. AFTER CASEY RATCHET HAD been killed and the uproar that ensued, the police force, with the help of the surrounding counties, would not allow anyone into Coalfield for two weeks. If you did not reside within the town of Coalfield, you could not enter the city limits except for deliveries of necessary items like food and gasoline. The governor of Tennessee declared a state of emergency. By this point there were documented sightings of the poster in every single state in the country, and in at least thirty other countries, and Coalfield was still papered over with them. On TV, ABC News ran a story about the posters. They reported that a man in Denver, Colorado, who had been suffering from terminal cancer had killed himself and left behind a note that consisted only of the lines that I had written earlier that summer. Someone in New York City was wheatpasting huge versions of the poster in Times Square and it had become a game for hipsters to take pictures of them before they were torn down. A woman in Hillsborough, North Carolina, said the lines came from an unpublished novel by her late husband, who had written hundreds of erotic novels under the pen name Dick Paine.

They interviewed our mayor, who said he was still convinced that it was the manifestation of the devil, and that he was hopeful that the strangers in the original black van would be found and brought to justice. Four years later, we'd find out that he had a second family in Knoxville, and that family would move to Coalfield and live with his first family in a weird harmony, and he would be the mayor for years and years after that, until he died of a massive heart attack while sitting in a dunking booth at the county fair.

—

I CAME HOME AND MY ARM HEALED. MY BROTHERS WERE TENTATIVE around me, kind even. I think they were a little shocked that I had survived something worse than anything they'd lived through. They had not realized that I was also invincible, I guess, and it made them wary of my power, of what I could do to them.

Hobart, who hobbled around on crutches because of his broken leg, both of us recovering, spent a fair amount of time with me while my mom was at work. We would drink huge glasses of sweet tea and take turns reading out loud to each other from Patricia Highsmith novels. I kind of grew to truly like him, how tender and sensitive he was once you got past the bluster of him.

He had quit the job with the newspaper and was unemployed, had basically moved in with us. I would read the classifieds section of the newspaper with him and circle jobs that looked interesting. One of them was to be a delivery driver for Schwan's, and Hobart applied and they sent back a catalog of their food. We'd spend a lot of time looking at ugly pictures of chicken Kiev and ice cream bars. We started checking for interesting sales, and we'd drive a few towns over to buy a bunch of VHS tapes of rare movies, ones I'd never even heard of but Hobart said were brilliant. He said he might open a video store in Coalfield, one with hard-to-find cult classics, and later on that is what he ended up doing, and even though it didn't make much money, he kind of became famous among collectors and film buffs, all those weird people on internet forums. He had a knack for finding stuff. He was generally clueless, but he was good at this.

One afternoon, after I'd read a section of *This Sweet Sickness*, we were making peanut butter sandwiches, and Hobart said, "I hated being a teenager."

"I don't hate it," I said, feeling a little affronted.

"Well, I did," he told me, looking so sad. "Not because I thought something better was coming. I just never felt right inside my own body."

"I feel that sometimes," I admitted.

"And then I got older, and, guess what? I still never felt right inside my body. I don't think I ever will. I kind of flamed out everywhere I went, always got a little less than what I thought I'd get. But I guess that's okay. I think maybe it's necessary to feel like you're not quite settled, or maybe for some people it's necessary."

"Even if you do feel settled," I suggested, "something could happen to ruin it."

"Yeah, that's true," he said, laughing. "I guess I just mean that sometimes your mom says that things will be better for you in the future. And I think they will, Frankie. I think you're really smart and I think you'll do fine. But I also think it's not so bad if you never quite feel right in this world. It's still worth hanging around. You just have to look harder to find the things you love."

"Okay," I said. I kind of wanted to hug him. I thought for a split second about telling him that I made the poster, but I knew I wouldn't. But the fact that I considered it made me realize that he could marry my mom and I'd be happy about it.

—

MY MOM MADE ME GO ON LONG WALKS THROUGH THE NEIGHborhood, to clear my head after so long in the house, and I would wave to Mr. Avery and he would wave back. And every time we made it back to our front door, my mom would hug me and say, "You're going to be okay, sweetie."

I never heard a word from Zeke. I knew there were so many reasons that he wouldn't contact me. He was terrified of the poster and what might happen if anyone found out. But I knew, more than that, he was ashamed that he'd hurt me, had done something awful. If he didn't check on me or apologize for what he'd done, he could pretend it hadn't happened.

In my head, I kept thinking about how he had pushed me away when I'd needed him, had pushed me down the freaking stairs, and maybe it was my own blindness, but I didn't believe it was on purpose. I know that I was making excuses for him, trying to ignore all the ways that his rage had pushed his life into bad places. I was protecting him because I guess I thought he needed it. And if I protected the person who hurt me, who had broken me, then I was stronger than he was and I was stronger than anyone who might try to hurt us more. And maybe that would bring him back.

I'd made the decision that I would forgive him, and I wouldn't apologize for that. And I'm not apologizing now. But after he left, I just wanted him to talk to me, to reach out, and I really believed it would go back to the way it was. But I couldn't be the one to call for him. It had to be him, I thought. And he wasn't going to do it.

It killed me. And even though I was getting better, I felt like I was dying. Coalfield felt empty. It felt lonelier than it had before the summer began, and it made me hate him a little because of it.

THERE WAS NOTHING ELSE TO DO, SO I WROTE THE NOVEL, finished it, and I made sure that my character, the evil genius, got away with it, that no one ever discovered what she'd done, what she was still doing, what she would never stop doing. She was invincible. She was a fugitive, goddammit, and the law was so skinny with hunger for her. I gave it to my mom, maybe to show her that I was getting better, or maybe because I had no one else who could acknowledge what I'd done. She loved it. "This is what you were doing all summer?" she asked, and I nodded, yes, of course, this and only this, and here is the proof of my last few months. She showed it to Hobart, who also loved it, and it made me feel, for the first time, that maybe it was dumb to be embarrassed about weird things if you were really good at them. Or not good. If they made you happy.

Of course, I kept putting up the poster. For the first one after the accident, I folded it up into a little bird, and I walked by myself in the morning heat to put the poster right in Zeke's grandmother's mailbox. After I shut the lid, I looked in the window, and I could see her on her sofa, watching TV, all alone. I left before she could see me, but I hoped that she'd find it, call Zeke's mother, and she and Zeke would drive right back to Coalfield. But nothing happened, or nothing happened that made any difference to me. Maybe I terrified the absolute shit out of Zeke's grandmother. I have no idea. Nothing reached me.

Sometimes, when I was alone, I'd go into the garage and make copies of the poster, using the original one. I had been the one who kept it. It was mine, the least that Zeke could do after he made me nearly die. I had the real one, the first one, and all of the power that was inside of it. Our blood, those stars in the sky. I'd make five copies at a time, just enough to make me feel like it was still mine.

My arm was in a cast when school started, but I didn't ask anyone to sign it. No one asked, either; it's not like I spent hours each day refusing the long line of well-wishers, armed with Sharpies, who wanted to leave a mark on me. In some ways, it made me more invisible, because people saw the cast, steered clear, and weren't even sure who the arm belonged to. I slid folded posters through the slits of random lockers. A few kids who wore their T-shirts of my poster to school, the bootleg ones they bought from Action Graphix, had to go back home and change and they were kind of legendary in those first few weeks of school.

One girl, Jenny Gudger, who I honestly had not noticed, either, wore the shirt three times and was suspended for a week. When she came back, I started sitting with her at lunch, and we'd sometimes talk about the poster. She'd been at camp most of the summer, so I liked telling her a version of what happened, pretending I was a bystander, an observer, and it was good practice, to know about the panic but not tell everything. And maybe we would have become friends, real friends, but before Christmas break, she got pregnant and her parents sent her to Atlanta to live with her aunt. I started skipping lunch and hanging out in the library instead, working on applications for college, planning my future. That was my plan, to imagine the future.

For the most part, the panic had subsided. It was like the epicenter of the disaster, where we were recovering, but the ripples of it, the seismic activity, were still reverberating farther and farther out into the world. But, honestly, no one in the pre-internet (or pre-internet-as-I-know-it-now) era could really get any consensus on who was responsible, and without deeper research, the origin was no longer important. It was just a thing that existed in the world now, and there was nothing that would change that.

With the triplets gone to college, my mom and I spent all our time together, Hobart shuffling around us, and I talked to them more and more about college, what I might want to do. We'd eat dinner and watch a movie and it was honestly the most like a family that I think I'd ever felt. I had survived something, something I'd made, and I wasn't sure that I was happy about it, but I wasn't sure what else could be done.

And then, these little flashes, I'd hear the phrase, my words, in someone else's voice in my head. Maybe Zeke's? Not mine. And I'd lock up, feel trapped, and I would say the line, in my own voice, in my head, and it would calm me. It was mine. I had made it. And I wouldn't let anyone else take it from me. *The edge is a shantytown filled with gold seekers. We are fugitives, and the law is skinny with hunger for us.* It had not finished. I was still a fugitive. We were still fugitives. And I would live the rest of my life certain of this. And I cannot tell you how happy it made me.

PART II

We Are Fugitives, and the Law Is Skinny with Hunger for Us

FALL 2017

Thirteen

JUST TWO WEEKS AFTER MAZZY BROWER HAD FIRST COLD-called my house and ruined my life, I was sitting in a booth at the Krystal in a town thirty minutes from where I lived, in Bowling Green. I'd dropped Junie off at school, gone home, and paced the house for three straight hours, the cat meowing and pacing right alongside me, occasionally getting caught between my feet, making me yell out curses. And then I'd texted my husband, who was at this point in the day deep inside the mouths of people we knew very well, cleaning and fixing their teeth, and I told him that I was going to meet someone who wanted to interview me about my writing. It was not an odd thing to assert, because I had written some books that were very popular, and because people sometimes talked to me, and so it was an easy lie.

Because, the thing is, I had never told my husband that I was responsible for the Coalfield Panic of 1996. I did not tell him that the T-shirt I sometimes wore, which I'd ordered from a very expensive clothing store in Toronto, had the exact phrase that I had written when I was sixteen.

Aaron knew I was from Coalfield, that I had been there during the panic, and we'd talked about it. But I had never told him the truth. Because when I met him, he was kind of a doofus and not that interesting to me as a romantic partner. He had been into teeth even when he was in college, and that seemed like something I didn't want to get involved in. He was interested in *my* teeth, actually, because my two front teeth had been badly repaired by a very inexpensive dentist who was not particularly good. And he acknowledged how bad the repair job was and said that someday, when he was a dentist, he would fix my messed-up teeth, free of charge, and so, you can see how unromantic that was, and you can understand why I wasn't going to tell him that I was responsible for a work of art that people thought was the product of Satan.

And then, one night, you make out with that guy because, even if he is interested mostly in your *teeth*, it's still more than most of the other guys in college have noticed about you. And then, after you make out, there's a small window where you can tell someone about your culture-altering poster, and I missed that window because I still wasn't thinking *I will marry this doofus who wants to fix my teeth and was, like, kind of licking my teeth while we made out*. And then we dated off and on, and each time it was off, I was thinking, *I am so glad I didn't tell him. I am so glad I did not show him the poster*, and then when it was on, I was thinking, *Just in case he forgets your birthday and instead goes to a comic book convention for a* second *time, don't show him that poster*, and then I was dancing with him at our wedding, and my mom was watching us and crying, and I knew that I couldn't spin away from him and then spin back and tell him that there was a boy, Zeke, and there was nothing romantic about it, that it wasn't like that, but I would never stop thinking about him and he was partially responsible for the trajectory of my entire life, and also, I was a fugitive and the law was skinny with hunger for me, all while Patsy Cline was singing "You Belong to Me" and someone was videotaping us. And then I fell in love with Aaron for real, who was weirder and more interesting than I'd first thought, and he was above all incredibly kind and gentle and he loved our daughter, and I thought, *What if I ruin this? What if the thing inside of me ruins everything and I lose it all?* So I didn't say a word. It stayed a secret. A secret that Mazzy Brower had somehow discovered.

When she showed up, I was shocked to realize that she was older than me. I had expected, with a name like *Mazzy*, that she was going to be some hipster girl from Brooklyn who was twenty, had graduated from Yale early, was somehow on staff at the *New Yorker*, and then I would find out that her grandfather was, I don't know, Dave Thomas, the Wendy's guy. But she was older than me; she was tall and slightly skeletal, with graying hair, and she had on this really amazing floral button-up shirt from the seventies. And this whole time, I was thinking, *I did not expect this*, and then she was standing over me, looking down at me in the booth of this fast-food place that sold tiny steamed burgers, and I said, "Hi," so quietly, I had no idea if she'd heard.

"Frankie?" she asked, but she knew it was me, of course. She'd found me.

"That's me," I said. "That is my name, yes."

"I'm Mazzy," she said. "Thanks so much for agreeing to meet with me. Do you think I could sit down? Could we talk?"

I wondered what it would feel like to say, "Hmm . . . no," and then stand up and get in my car and whip it into traffic, nearly causing a massive accident, and then never talk to her.

"Sure," I said, "I mean, I feel like we'd better talk."

She slid into the other side of the booth and then stood right back up. "Could I get something to eat? I'm starving."

"Yeah, sure, that's fine. I would, well, maybe I'd have picked somewhere else if I knew we were going to eat."

"This place isn't good?" she asked.

"No, it's really good," I said. "It's really good . . . in my opinion."

"Well, if you say it's good, I'm going to go with that," she replied, and she stalked off to order. And then I knew I didn't want to sit there while she ate, staring at her, so I went and ordered ten Krystals, large fries, two Corn Pups, and a large Dr Pepper. It would be good, I thought, to feel slightly sick as everything changed.

While we ate, she explained who she was, which was nice to hear, because for some reason, I had not even looked her up online. Why had I not looked her up online? I think I wanted to keep believing that it wasn't real, that I would show up and no one would be there to meet me and I could walk right back into my old life.

She was an art critic, and she focused mostly on lesser-known New York artists, mostly painters, mostly women, but she had discovered a painter named Henry Roosevelt Wilson, and was writing a book about him. He was from upstate New York, a place called Keene, and had lived on a farm with his wife, Henrietta Wilson (Henry and Henrietta, holy god), and he'd mostly painted these ghostlike portraits on salvaged doors that he purchased at estate sales. He was a fairly minor painter in his lifetime, though he had been in some group exhibitions in New York and San Francisco. He had also been a pitcher and played Double-A for a farm team of the Milwaukee Brewers before he broke his arm trying to climb into a second-story window after curfew. His mother and father had been murdered in a botched robbery when he was seven, and he had lived in an orphanage until he was fourteen, and it was at the orphanage where he had started painting on doors.

Mazzy showed me some images of his work, which were indeed ghostlike, the figures tall and narrow and almost turning to mist in front of you. But they were beautiful. And then she showed me a photo of Henry, who was, holy moly, so handsome. Crazy handsome. Like a farmhand-who-wins-a-modeling-competition-and-then-gets-to-marry-a-princess kind of handsome, with curly brown hair and bright blue eyes and rippling muscles under a loose linen shirt. If you looked like that, I decided, everyone else probably looked like they were dissolving in front of you. How could you paint anyone who wasn't as pretty as you, so you made it up to them by turning them into ghosts so they wouldn't feel too bad.

"So," Mazzy continued, "I went to see Henrietta when I began to research Henry's life, and she was incredibly reluctant to talk about Henry, really protective of him, and there wasn't much information available about him, and so I had to really charm her, to tell her how much I loved his paintings, and I think she eventually realized that I could bring her husband's work to the larger world, which had, you know, mostly ignored him when he was alive. I rented an apartment in Keene, above this old general store, and I'd meet with her every few days. And then, one day, she just kind of, I don't know, decided that she wasn't long for this world and Henry was dead, and it was okay to tell me everything. And so she did."

Henry, Mazzy informed me, had been gay, and Henrietta had known this going into the relationship, but she liked him and he was sweet and he had a huge farm that she loved. And it was nearly impossible for Henry to have many lasting relationships with men in the area, so he was hers more than he was someone else's. At some point, he met Randolph Avery during a gallery exhibition in Los Angeles, and the two of them formed an intense friendship that lasted the rest of their lives, though it wasn't physical. Or at least Henrietta had assured Mazzy that it wasn't. And they stayed in close contact until Avery died. Avery, I knew, had died of AIDS, only a few years after that summer in Coalfield.

I learned about it—well, not that he died of AIDS, because no one would have talked about that in Coalfield, even in the nineties—when I was in college, making out with Aaron. My mom called to tell me that he had died. She said that he'd passed away in his sleep, and I immediately wondered about my backpack, if he had kept it, if his sister would find it. I had been too embarrassed to retrieve it when I still lived in Coalfield, wanted to preserve the possibility that our entire interaction had been a dream. But now, knowing someone else might stumble upon it, I was so nervous, because my backpack had my initials sewn onto it, something my mom had paid ten dollars extra to get, and that seemed like the dumbest way possible to have this discovered. "What do you think will happen to his belongings?" I asked my mom, and immediately I thought, *What the fuck are you doing, Frankie?*

"What, sweetie?" she asked.

"Uhhhh, hmm, um, well, like, do you think, like, there will be an estate sale or anything? Or will a museum want them? He was an artist, right? Might be some neat stuff. I might come back to Coalfield to bid on something."

"Honey, did you smoke weed?" she asked. "A museum is not going to take Mr. Avery's stuff. He was not that famous of an artist."

And then I felt really sad because I did want to get my backpack so I wouldn't get discovered, but I also wanted his haori, to wear it as I walked across campus. But instead, I just told my mom that I had to go study. And we never talked about it again. As far as I know, my backpack is still somewhere in his sister's house. I now wondered if Mazzy had found it, but I was getting way ahead of myself. I had eaten seven of the burgers already. I needed to slow down. I had to let Mazzy tell me what she knew, so I could figure out what she didn't know.

Mazzy said, "And finally, after Henrietta had unearthed from various basements and barns, and even a few friends' houses, every single painting of Henry's in existence, she then gave me this huge bundle of letters from Randolph Avery. I mean, they must have written to each other at least once or twice a week until Avery died."

I imagined that, somewhere in his sister's house in Coalfield, all of Mr. Avery's letters from Henry were hidden away, perhaps in the same place as my book bag.

"So I've been reading them, one by one, making notations, cross-checking them. I mean, a lot of it is about the fact that Randolph loved the Dodgers and Henry loved the Yankees, and so there are a *lot* of baseball names I had to go over. But I got to the summer of 1996, and I was interested because Randolph was regularly updating Henry on the panic, and I'm sure you know that a fair number of people suspected that he might have been responsible for it."

"Yes, I had heard that. It makes sense," I said. I mean, I had told her on the phone two weeks ago that it was me, but maybe I could still figure a way out of it. Randolph Avery had hidden the evidence the first time, and I wondered, now that he was dead, if he might just keep hiding it for me.

"Well, but no," Mazzy said, looking slightly confused. "Right? Because it was you."

"Let me hear more of what you know," I said.

She told me that several of the letters mentioned me. She pulled out a photocopy of one of the letters, and she waited for me to move my tray, all those little empty hamburger boxes, so she could place it in front of me. I was immediately struck by how messy Mr. Avery's handwriting was, not the elegant long strokes, the flowing cursive, that I imagined from an artist. It was printed, scratched into the paper, and then I remembered, *Oh, he was dying*, and that's cruel, of course, but it made sense. I don't know why it mattered to me that Mr. Avery's handwriting be beautiful, but I think if you wear a Japanese kimono around Coalfield, then you should also have beautiful, flowing handwriting that looks like calligraphy.

"So," Mazzy said, interrupting the weird stuff going on in my head, "this is what's important. He mentions to Henry that he's figured out who did it. He says, right here, 'I might be the only person in the world, Henry, who knows this for a fact.' And then, look: 'It's my neighbor, a girl, a teenager named Frankie Budge.'"

I read it along with her, watching her finger move across the text. It made me gasp when I saw my own name. He had told. He had told someone.

"And that's you," Mazzy said.

"It's my name, yes," I admitted. I kept reading, and I could see Mazzy tense up for a second. *Henry, it's astonishing. This plain little country girl, so painfully awkward and dull*—"Okay, wait, keep reading," Mazzy said—*might be the greatest artist I've ever known. She puts my work to shame. Your work, I'm sorry to say, love, as well.*

She took the letter back and put it away. "He talks about your . . . your accident. He calls it something else, but, anyways, he mentions the posters, and he says that he closely observed them against the very first ones, and he had often noticed you walking around at strange hours, and he's certain it was you. And that you told him it was you."

"And this is how you found out?" I asked her. "Like, you weren't trying to find out? You just wanted to write a book about this painter that no one has ever heard of?"

"I mean . . . yes."

"And because that old lady gave you these secret letters, you now know that I made the poster?"

"Well, I told you, I'm almost one hundred percent certain that it was you. I've read your books, especially the one that you said you wrote in high school, and the main character talks a lot about going to *the edge* and there's some imagery that feels very similar to what's in the poster. I just . . . I mean, I honestly think it's one of the most amazing things. I just . . . It's you. You told me it was you. On the phone. It's you."

The edge, the edge, the edge, the edge . . . the edge is a shantytown filled with gold seekers. We are fugitives, and the law is skinny with hunger for us. I said it to myself, exactly in my own voice, and then I looked at Mazzy.

"I made it," I finally said. "Yes, one hundred percent. I wrote it."

"You have proof?" she said.

I'd brought the proof. I needed it to be as close to me as possible when I met with this woman who was trying to open up my life and unsteady me and possibly change everything that I'd done to make life possible. I reached into my backpack and I got out the polyester film folder, a museum-grade, top-quality archival sleeve. And I showed it to her, and she made this little sound, like someone had stepped on her chest. "This is the original," I told her. "The first one. Everything came from this one."

"This is the one?"

"And that's my blood," I said, pointing to the stars.

"Your blood?" she said, her eyes widening. I nodded.

She looked at the poster, the first time that anyone except me had looked at this poster in twenty years. I thought it might melt other people's faces off, blind them, turn them into statues. But the archival polyester must have been protecting other humans from disaster, I imagined.

Mazzy leaned back against the hard curve of the bench, looked up at the ceiling. And then she smiled. She smiled, all her beautiful teeth, nothing like mine, nothing like Zeke's, and she touched my hand. "This is amazing," she finally said.

"I'm scared," I said. "It's . . . it's just very complicated."

"You said the same thing on the phone that day. You said it was complicated. What do you mean?"

"What do I mean?" I replied. "I mean . . . it's complicated. I can't quite explain it all."

"Did someone else make it with you? Did you have help? Your brothers, maybe?"

"My brothers?" I said, snorting involuntarily with laughter. "Not my brothers, no way." I thought about my brothers. The triplets had dropped out of college and then worked in kitchens for years and now co-owned a restaurant in Charleston, South Carolina, one that made modern twists on southern dishes, and it had appeared in tons of magazines, on the Food Network, and it kept them so busy that I almost never saw them. None of them had married, no children, just three feral boys constantly beating each other up and dating all manner of hip women with tattoos and getting drunk in between appearances on the *Today* show making saltine cracker toffee or Cheerwine barbecue sauce. They were really into jujitsu now, woodworking, dipping a little into doomsday prep. It was like they made a world unto themselves and they were stunned whenever they saw me, the one who was and wasn't a part of them.

No, definitely not the triplets.

"Who, then?" she asked.

I looked around. The lunch rush was over; the dining room of the Krystal was totally empty except for us. It was the longest I'd sat in a fast-food restaurant since I was a teenager.

"I don't know," I said.

"I want to write about this, Frankie," she told me. "I mean, I *am* going to write about it. An article for the *New Yorker*. You can imagine that they are very interested in the story, but no one knows anything yet. Just me. And you. And . . . well, anyone else who knows. But I need you to talk to me about it. I need your help to make sense of it."

"It doesn't make any sense," I told her. "Like, seriously, are you kidding me? Do you think I had any idea what would happen? It makes no sense."

"I think it can," she said. "If you let me help you."

"I need some time to tell people. I need—fuck—I need to tell my husband. I need to tell my mom. I just . . . I need a little time to figure things out."

"But then you'll talk to me?" she asked. "You'll come forward?"

"Okay," I finally said. "Okay, yes. I did it. I'll tell people that I did it."

She handed me a card. "This is my email and my phone. I know you already have it, but here, if you think of anything, write it down or call me. If you go anywhere and you need me to come with you, I will come with you."

I imagined this woman I'd just met coming with me to sit on a couch next to my mom while I said, "I made that thing that made a lot of people lose their minds and also inadvertently caused a few people we knew to die," and my mom going, "Oh, sweetie, we'll need to talk about that, but does your friend here want, like, something to drink? Or some sandwiches? Does she want pizza? Frankie? Frankie? Are you listening? *Does your friend want pizza?*"

Mazzy stared at me for a second. "Could I have your cell phone number? I've only ever called your home phone. It's just so we can stay in touch." I had a feeling that she suspected I might immediately get on a plane to some random country and she'd be left with an article that no one wanted to publish. I think she was very smart to suspect that.

I looked at her card and used my phone to send a text to her, and she nodded and then added me to her contacts. We stood up. I still had a Corn Pup left to eat, and I was about to reach for it when Mazzy asked, "Where did it come from?"

I was looking at the mini corn dog, distracted, but then tried to focus. "The poster?" I asked.

"The words, yeah, that phrase," she said. "Where did it come from?"

"Me," I said, not sure what else to say.

She looked at me for a few seconds, and I knew she was repeating the phrase in her head. I could hear every single syllable inside her mind, the entire utterance, because I knew what it sounded like so clearly.

"Let's talk soon," she said, and I agreed, and as soon as she left, I dipped the corn dog in mustard and ate it in two bites.

Fourteen

AFTER HIGH SCHOOL, I GOT A SCHOLARSHIP AND ENDED UP AT a small liberal arts college in Kentucky, which is where I met Aaron. And I made friends. I felt myself expand into those open spaces, to hang out with people who had been like me in high school and now were surprised that, holy shit, they could revise themselves into someone who was a little cooler. I was an English major and sometimes I shocked my professors by having read some of the books already. They were impressed, and that made them give me a little extra attention, and that made me feel so grown-up that I decided I'd devote my four years to doing whatever they said.

Senior year, I did an independent study with a cranky old lit professor named Dr. Burr Blush, who was retiring at the end of the year and had not, to my knowledge, taught a course that you could register for in the past decade. He had a huge office in the library, one with *three* sofas (which he later told me were reserved for separate uses: 1. socializing, 2. reading, and 3. sleeping), and I never saw him anywhere else on campus, as if he teleported into the room each morning and then went back through some kind of wormhole to his home. I had searched him out specifically because I wanted to show someone the novel I'd written that summer in Coalfield, and I did not want it to be anyone who had a connection to me, a professor who would then think, *I simply cannot write a letter of recommendation for a girl who writes Nancy Drew fan fiction*. If it was awful, the only person who would know would be an old deranged man who would most likely die in his office on the day of his retirement.

Through a little research in the library, I found out that Dr. Blush, who, when he was actually teaching students, specialized in nineteenth-century American literature, had also written a novel called *Huckleberry Finn in Russia*, where Huck ends up winning the affections of Olga Nikolaevna, the daughter of Emperor Nicholas I, and is chased by the Imperial Guard all over the continent. It was a deeply insane book, with Tom Sawyer at one point showing up with a pet Siberian tiger to help Huck and Olga escape from a burning building before completely disappearing from the story. It ends with Huck becoming the czar of the Russian Empire and deciding to conquer all of Europe. As soon as I finished it, I thought, *Dr. Blush will love my evil Nancy Drew novel.*

I think my presence at his office door shocked him in such a way that he signed the form just to get me to leave, but I also gave him a typed copy of the manuscript, and I did not see him again, despite knocking on his door, for more than a month. Then, just as I'd given up, I received a letter at the campus post office, on real stationery, wherein Dr. Blush invited me to meet with him in his office, where he proceeded to tell me that he thought the book was really quite good. "Subversive!" he kept saying. "So strangely subversive, you understand? It was intentional, right?" and I proclaimed that it was entirely intentional, hoping he wouldn't keep pressing me on it. He admitted that he had read the Hardy Boys and Nancy Drew novels to his eight children, and he had a fondness for them but also an intense irritation with how good everyone in them was. "It's unnatural for two brothers to not, at some point, beat the absolute shit out of each other over some ridiculous slight, don't you think?" he asked me, and I guess it would have been nice to see Frank throw Joe off a balcony over a broken microscope.

When he handed me the manuscript back, it had been line-edited, everything written in neat penmanship with red ink, and he said that I would get an A if I just made the suggested revisions, mostly grammatical because, he stressed, my grammar was quite terrible. The class was done, and I spent the rest of the semester sitting on his sofa every Tuesday and Thursday, the one reserved for entertaining, and I would do my homework and study, and he would either read or nap, and sometimes we would drink tea and he would talk about literature, admitting that he understood very little of it, and he was kind and lovely. At the end of the year, he told me that his grandson's wife was a literary agent for a boutique agency in New York, and he had sent her the book, which she loved, and she was certain that she could sell it and it would be a breakout series for teens. He handed me a card with her information on it. I was crying, which he did not seem to notice, and before I could hug him, he went back to lie down on his sleeping couch. If someone had walked into that office at that moment, to find Dr. Blush snoring on his sofa and me bawling so hard that I was hiccupping, I cannot imagine what they would have assumed. By the end of the summer after graduation, I'd signed a two-book deal with a major publishing house. Because of this old man who did end up dying five months after he retired, which made me cry all over again, his kindness before he disappeared from my life, which was not how people usually left me or I left them.

As Frances Eleanor Budge, I had written four of those books featuring Evie Fastabend causing chaos throughout the town of Running Hollow, both loving and hating her father and sister (their mother long dead). And they were all bestsellers, and lots of girls dressed up like Evie Fastabend for Halloween, and, well, again, it was deeply strange to watch this thing I had made in my room in Coalfield that summer spread out into the world. There was always talk of a TV series or movie, but it never quite happened, which was fine with me. I didn't want it to be that real.

A few years ago, as Frankie Budge, I published an adult novel called *Sisters with the Same First Name*, which was about a woman who learns that her long-lost father is dying and travels cross-country, picking up all twelve of her half sisters, all born to different mothers, who each share her first name, on their way to his deathbed. And it did *not* do well, sold poorly, and though the reviews were positive, I could tell that maybe I'd tried too hard to write about my own life, had made it too explicitly autobiographical, and it had gotten messed up in the execution. I'd been embarrassed in the interviews and events when I started to talk about my dad, ancient history. It was fine now. It was a good enough book. I had wondered if my father might read it and contact me, but I had not seen or heard from him since he'd come to my college graduation, when Brian tried to karate kick him before the ceremony even started, and all of us decided, I guess without saying it, that we did not ever need to see each other again. His daughter Frances, who looks nothing like me, is very pretty and has a very active social media presence; she works for a publicity firm in Chicago and the two of us have never exchanged a single word. I think if we met in real life, one of us would explode, would simply cease to exist. I don't even know if she has any idea who I am. I keep hoping that she will get married, will take the man's last name, and maybe then, *maybe*, I wouldn't hate her quite as much as I do, as petty as that is.

I guess what I'm trying to say is that I lived in the world. I was famous in the way you can be as a writer of a book kids loved for a brief period of their lives, and I navigated all kinds of situations where things I'd made were discussed and considered, and sometimes people asked me to join those discussions. I didn't mind.

And I had a really great husband and a kid who was lovely and beautiful, and I volunteered twice a week at the elementary school library to read to kids who did not give a shit and just wanted to fight over the pillows they got to lie on, and I visited schools in the neighboring counties to talk to teenagers about writing, and it was an entire life that I'd made. But I guess the other thing is that I had built that life over another life, this secret life, this secret thing, and I had told myself that this would all work as long as I kept my life on top of that secret, if I weighed it down so it stayed deep inside of me. And when something comes back, when it reappears, when it emerges from that place inside of you, it takes up real space in the world that you've made. And I wasn't sure how much space it needed, if it would push me so far outside of that life that I'd have to start over, become someone else.

That night, I had Junie's babysitter take her out to see a movie, and after Aaron came home from work, I told him that I needed to tell him something. My whole body was kind of vibrating; my skin felt tingly.

"You look a little sick," Aaron said, frowning. "Are you okay?"

"I just listen—" I said, and he instantly stiffened.

"Did someone die?" he blurted out. "Did your mom die? Wait, did *my* mom die? Is that why you sent Junie out with Bea?"

"No, god, Aaron, I'm sorry. No, nobody died. No one is dead. No one is dying, either. It's nothing like that. Jeez, you ran to that so fast."

"You just had that look," he said, still suspicious of me. "Like someone had died. You looked like my mom when she told me that our dog got hit by a car."

"Well, thank god, it's nothing like that. This is just my face, you know? My normal face."

"You're really pale," he said, inspecting my face. "You're sweating."

"Shit, you're making this worse," I told him. "Do you want a beer or something? Do you think that would relax you?"

"I think you'd better tell me what it is," he said, "'cause you're freaking me out a little bit."

"Okay, well, I met with this woman today, and she wants to write about me for the *New Yorker*, and so—"

"Oh, shit, Jesus, Frankie, it's good news? Why were you acting like that? This is great! Is it about the Evie books? Or your novel?"

"No," I said, "it's not about the books."

"Oh," he replied. He was smiling, but I could see that his mind was working, trying to figure out why anyone would want to talk to me if it wasn't about Evie Fastabend and her evil mind. "Well, then what?"

"She wants to talk to me about the Coalfield Panic," I finally said.

"Is it, like, an oral history, then? Frankie, jeez, I'm confused, and I wish you'd just say what—"

"I did it," I said, screaming a little. "I made it happen. Back then. I made the poster. I wrote those words."

"Shut up," he said, frowning. "Frankie, you would get in a ton of trouble if you lied about that. She's a reporter, so, like, she would—"

"I really did. I really did. Back then, that summer. I wrote that phrase, and I made the poster and I hung it up all over town, and then things got really weird, and it was too late to do anything about it. And so I just didn't tell anyone, ever."

"You didn't tell *me*," he said. "You didn't tell me about this? What the hell?"

I reached for him and he let me, which was a kindness, to let me touch him. I hugged him. "I didn't tell *anyone*, Aaron. Do you understand? I couldn't."

"Well, you must have told someone, because this lady knows, right?"

"It's complicated," I told him. "She kind of knew, and then she asked me, and I said yes. And now she is going to write about it. And everybody is going to know."

"Well, now, shit, wait. You know, Marcus is a lawyer, so we should ask him about it first."

"Your brother does immigration law, Aaron. He wouldn't know the first thing about something like this."

"Well, he knows the language, right? He could do, like, a cease-and-desist. Or sue for defamation of character."

"But, Aaron, do you understand? You heard me, right? I did it. I did do it. I made it. The edge? You know about the edge, right? I wrote that. I made it."

"Well, it feels really defamatory to bring that shit up now," he said, trying so hard to protect me, which made me feel much worse. "It feels libelous or whatever to bring up something you did as a juvenile. Shouldn't that be sealed, you know? The record of it should be sealed, because you weren't eighteen."

Junie would be home in less than an hour. We were not going to spend that time on the internet typing *mass hysteria legal responsibility juvenile statute of limitations* and reading twenty pages of results. It was too late for that. The story had already happened. I'd already written it.

"I think you should talk to Jules," he said suddenly, referring to my literary agent. "I mean, you need to let the publisher know, too. Because they might not be too jazzed about this."

"I mean, I will tell them, I guess, but I don't care that much right now."

"It could harm your sales, for sure," he said. "Maybe they won't want to publish the next one."

"Okay, I know this is a lot to handle. But, like, you think my publisher is going to be upset that the lady who writes about a diabolical teenage genius girl who causes chaos in her small town is the person responsible for that whole panic?"

"You're kind of a role model figure—"

"I'm not at all. I am not that famous in any way. Okay, Aaron? Focus. Do you understand? I'm telling you now. Not anyone else. I'm telling you. I should have told you sooner, but I think, a few days from now, maybe, you'll think about all of this and realize how fucked up it would have been to tell you at literally any point in our relationship, how there was never a good time to tell. Okay? And this is *not a good time*, either, I get it. But it's happening, and I'm telling you."

"But, what exactly are you telling me?"

"Aaron, just, I made it, okay? I really did. I have the original poster, the first one I ever made. And then I made, like, hundreds and hundreds of copies and I put them up and then things got weird and then it was out of my hands."

"I've seen those posters in town," he said suddenly. "I saw one on the bulletin board at the library. Remember? I told you I'd seen it. And how weird that was?"

"I remember, yeah."

"Did you put that up?"

"Did I what now?" I asked, stalling. "Put what up?"

"The poster! Did you put that specific poster up on the bulletin board of our local library, Frankie?"

"Yeah," I replied, "I did."

"So you still do it," he said. "So you kind of, like, never stopped doing it."

"I guess not," I said. "Not as much as before, but, yeah, I still do it."

"Why?" he asked, almost shouting. "That's so messed up, Frankie. And . . . and you have that T-shirt and you wear it around the house."

"Well, Jesus, it's not like *the fucking shirt* is evil or anything, Aaron. I didn't bring some cursed object into the house."

"You did, though," he said. "Kind of, you did. You have that poster."

"Okay, I thought you'd be mad that I hadn't told you before, but it sounds like you're mad that the physical object is in our house. Which is very weird."

"It's all weird!" he said. Aaron could get shouty when he was confused, like if he raised his voice, the world would understand that it needed to clarify some shit before things got out of hand. "I *am* mad that you didn't tell me, that you lied to me, but I *am also mad* that you keep putting the poster up and you have it in the house, and you seem obsessed with something that happened twenty years ago."

"It happened to *me*, though," I said. "It happened to me, so I *am* obsessed with it. It's confusing. I can't explain it all in thirty minutes and then everything will be fine. But, Aaron, and I need you to understand, okay? I don't feel bad. I don't feel bad that I made it. And I am never going to feel bad that I made it."

"Do you feel bad that you never told me?" he asked, and he looked like he was going to cry.

"I do. Of course I do. But I never told *anyone*. I never told my mom, okay? I never told anyone else about it. But, like, would you not have married me?"

Aaron didn't say anything.

"Aaron?"

"I don't know how to say it. It's like . . . I think it would have been better if you said you'd cheated on me. It would make more sense, you know? You've done something, and it is going to change our lives, whether I want it to or not, and I don't really know how to express how freaking mad I am about it."

"I understand that you are mad, and I know that you have every ri—"

"And I feel angry that, if this woman hadn't found out, you never would have told me. I would have died and not known."

"I am so sorry. I really am." I was about to ask him if he'd ever done anything that he'd regretted before, to get him to understand, but I knew his answer would be something like stealing a pack of gum when he was six, because he was so lovely and honest and had never lied to me about anything. And I had made people die from insanity. I just stopped trying to explain myself.

"And, I hate this, but I guess for as long as we live, I'll know that there was this thing you were going to keep hidden from me. And I guess I'll never know if there's more."

I made a weird sound, like I was testing to see if I was still breathing. I was.

"Is there more?" he asked.

"More what?" I made the sound again.

"Is there more that you need to tell me?" he asked, and I could see on his face that he was thinking, *I know there is more that you need to tell me. This is a test, Frankie.*

And of course there was. There was Zeke, and there was everything that happened that summer, all the details that were going to freak him out. There was more, of course there was.

"There *is* more," I told him, "but I can't handle it right now. I mean, I can tell you more, and I will tell you more, but I need some time to figure this out."

"On your own," he said, growing angry. "All by yourself."

"Kind of?" I replied. "You keep something a secret this long, it takes a little while to untangle it. I just need you to be patient with me."

"You're not leaving us, are you?" he asked, and it looked like he might start crying. "You're not going to go somewhere else and never come back?"

"No, god no. Aaron, no. You and Junie are the only things that I care about."

"The poster," he said.

"You and Junie are the only *people* I care about," I corrected. "I will never, ever, ever leave you."

"Okay," he finally said, taking a deep breath.

"But I am going to go away for, like, *a little while.*"

"Frankie, Jeeeee-sus Christ," he said.

"I need to clear up some things. I have to go back to Coalfield, you know? I have to tell my mom. I have to talk to this writer lady and make sure she gets all the details right."

"Okay," he said again. He looked so defeated.

This was the thing. I had kind of fucked up, but I had admitted it. And now, if he wanted to keep me, if he wanted to keep our life as it was, he would have to let me fuck things up a little more. But, like, this was marriage, right? This was love? I hoped it was.

I didn't want to think about what came next, honestly. I had always depended on the fact that Aaron thought I was good. I was a good mother and a good partner and a good person. And if he didn't think that, I wasn't sure what I'd do.

And this is when it hit me, the rest of our lives. I wanted to be with him for the rest of my life, not just right now, but forever. Days would go by sometimes when he was the only adult I talked to in real life, and I realized that part of why I didn't care about the rest of the world was because he gave me what I needed. And maybe I had ruined it. But I had to do this. I had to let the story reach the end, and then I'd come back and I'd hope that I could tell other stories.

"Junie is going to be home in, like, five minutes. Bea texted a while back," I told him.

"Don't tell her yet," he said.

"She wouldn't understand one bit of it," I said.

"I want you to act like it's all fine," he said. "I want you to sleep in our bed, okay? I don't want you to go to the guest room and be dramatic and make everything worse. I said it was okay for now, so you have to be normal. You have to be good for us."

"I wasn't going to go sleep in the guest room," I said.

"Well, *I'm* not going to sleep in the guest room."

"It's not a great bed," I admitted.

"Do you love me?" he asked.

"I do," I said, without hesitation, and it was nice to answer a question that didn't require constant adjustment to my brain. "I do, and you know I do."

"Okay," he said. "I believe you." But then he paused for a few seconds and I wondered if he was doubting me. I was just about to say something when he held up his hand.

"I'm trying to remember the phrase," he said. "I'm trying to remember the exact phrase."

"The edge is—"

"No," he said, "I don't want you to say it. Just . . . okay, yeah, the edge is a sh—" and then he was just mouthing the rest of the words, nodding, like it was a spell, which it was.

He looked up at me. "You made that up?" he said.

"I did."

"Your teenage brain did that?" he asked.

"It did," I admitted.

And when Junie burst into the room, holding a half-full box of Milk Duds, absolutely zooted on sugar and instantly explaining the plot of the movie they just saw, I thought, *Oh, thank god*. The chaos of our daughter, so lovely and beautiful, I would always be grateful for it, how she required us to keep living, to keep moving forward, just so she didn't leave us in her dust. I listened to her explain the movie, not a single word of it making the slightest bit of sense, but I listened as hard as I could, like if I tried hard enough, I would truly understand.

Fifteen

MY MOM WAS WAITING FOR ME ON THE FRONT PORCH WHEN I pulled into the driveway. She looked so beautiful, had let her hair go entirely silver and kept it short. She was wearing a camouflage Adidas tracksuit and the craziest sneakers, tropical snakeskin high-tops that I knew probably cost more than two hundred dollars. After all the kids moved out of the house, my mom ended up getting a really lucrative job with the Tennessee Department of Transportation, and she also got into collecting sneakers, which she could never really explain to me. "They look nice, don't you think?" she'd say, holding up a pair of men's Nike Terminators in a size too large for her to ever be able to wear them that she'd bought on eBay. She said people in town always commented on her sneakers, especially teenagers, and that made her feel good about herself.

She waved to me, and I waved back. I'd told her that I needed to visit for a few days, to talk to her about an article that someone was writing about me, and that they might need to talk to her as well. "Ooh, okay, exciting, I guess," she'd said, though she wasn't sure why I had to come back to Coalfield to do it. But she let me come. And here I was.

It wasn't like I never came home. We visited my mom at least six times a year, and she came to see Junie in Kentucky when she had free time. Hobart had died of a heart attack when I was in my late twenties, and they had really loved each other, I think, or at the very least, she had loved him more than she'd loved my dad. She had recently been dating a new guy, Hank, a former college soccer coach, who was very kind to my mother and clearly loved her, but they didn't live together. Every time I saw Hank, he had a bag of my books that he wanted me to sign for gifts to various family members and friends, which made me like him quite a bit.

"Come on in, sweetie," she said. "I've got coffee or sweet tea. I've got, like, thirty different kinds of Little Debbies."

"I'm good," I said, and we walked into the living room and sat down.

"Tell me what's going on," she said. "It sounded important. You never come here by yourself anymore."

I felt so shaky, like maybe the rest of my life would be tracking people down and telling them this secret. Or, no, that's what the article would do for me. What I was doing now was a kind of gift for myself, to tell the people I loved, to prepare them, to give them time to forgive me. *After* the article, the rest of my life would be awkwardly running into people I once knew and then watching them silently consider how deeply disturbed I was.

"Sweetie?" she said. "Is everything okay?"

"You know the panic?" I asked. "The reporter is writing about it."

"Oh dear," my mom said, tugging on the sleeves of her camo tracksuit, "oh my."

"Yeah, and, so, she's been talking to me about it."

"Talking to you?" my mom asked. "Just you?"

"Well, I guess maybe lots of people," I amended, "but mostly me."

"Okay. So, she's writing about the panic. And that was, you know, more than twenty years ago, but okay."

"And, she's talking to me, because I was the one who did it," I said. I needed to just say it. After Aaron, who thought his mom was *dead*, I realized I needed to be pretty forthright about this thing.

"Frankie?" she said, looking at me, her eyes watering.

"I made the poster," I told her. "I wrote those words. I made it up."

"Oh, sweetie," she said, and she looked so sad for me, like she was in pain to see me in pain, and then she said, "I knew that already."

"What now?" I said. She wasn't in pain, I realized. She was *embarrassed for me*.

"Frankie? I know. I knew then. I've always known. Well, I mean, not always, not at the beginning, but I've known for a really long time."

"But you didn't know," I said. "You had no idea. You thought it was the triplets."

"At first, yeah, of course, but then I figured it out. You were so strange that summer; I mean, even before you tried to kill yourself in the car—"

"That's not what happe—"

"Okay, well, I mean, you were so strange, more than usual, and I figured it out. Honey, how would I not have known? It was you."

"Well, yeah, that's what I'm telling you. It was me."

"I know."

"Oh god, Mom," I said.

"It was you and that boy that you had a crush on. It was . . . oh my god, the name just flew out of my head. His mom played the violin. I went to school with her. Jesus, I don't remember her name, either."

"His name was Zeke," I said. "It was me and Zeke."

"Yes, I know."

I wished she'd stop saying that she knew. She had short-circuited my brain a little bit. I was prepared to reveal this secret, ask for her forgiveness for not telling her, and then try to protect her from the fallout. And instead, she was sitting there on her sofa, waiting for me to catch up.

"We had a Xerox machine in our garage, sweetie," she said, softly, like I was six years old.

"But it was broken," I told her. "The triplets broke it."

"I know, which is why I didn't quite realize it at first. But once it got really bad, I would check the boxes of copy paper and it was always less than before."

"I didn't know if you remembered that we had that copier," I said. "Why didn't you tell me before? Why didn't you tell me that summer, after people died? Why didn't you make me stop?"

"Well, it did take me a while to figure it out, because you had confused me by liking a boy for the first time in your entire damn life, and then, crazy things had already happened, that boy fell off the water tower. And why in the world would I want to make you feel bad about that? You never mentioned it, and so I didn't, either."

"The whole time you've known," I said.

"And, sweetie, maybe I would have said something if you'd messed up your life. If you'd never been able to recover from that summer, I would have told you that it wasn't your fault, any of it, and that it was beautiful, I think, what you and Zeke made. But you got married, and you had Junie, and you're a published author, and you're a success. So I didn't need to say anything. And you didn't say anything, so I hoped that you'd forgotten about it, or put it behind you."

"I did not put it behind me, though," I admitted, and then I started crying. "I think about it every day. I say it every day, three or four times a day."

"Well, you're still alive. You made it. It's okay," my mom said, and now she was crying.

"Did Hobart know?" I asked. It suddenly seemed important.

"He had no clue, sweetie," she said. "You think Hobart, god rest his beautiful soul, would have figured it out? My god, no. Just me."

"And it's okay?" I asked.

"What's okay?" she replied.

"If I tell people now. Well, I mean this lady is going to tell people, and it's going to come out. I want to know that it's okay with you. You're still here in Coalfield. I worry people might hate you."

"Hate me?" she said. "It was twenty years ago, and I was a single mom raising four insane children. No, it's fine. I get some leeway on this."

"People got killed, though," I said.

"You didn't kill them, sweetie. You made a thing. And people went absolutely crazy, and they did strange things and some people died. I mean, I wish it hadn't happened. I wish you had maybe written it in a diary and that was that, but it's okay. It was beautiful, and then somebody else, the rest of the world, made it not beautiful."

"You'll be okay?" I asked.

"I'm the grandmother who wears Air Jordans, sweetie. It's fine. I'll be fine. Will *you* be okay?"

"Who knows?" I answered. "Aaron is so confused. Junie won't understand and won't care, but maybe later she'll wonder. I don't . . . I mean, I don't really know anyone else. I have friends, and they'll be super polite about it and a little weirded out, but I just really want you and Aaron and Junie, the only people I love, honestly, to not be hurt because I made this thing."

"Again, when you were sixteen, sweetie. It's fine. It's okay." She looked at me for a few seconds. "I honestly thought we'd never talk about this. I figured we would both die without ever telling anyone."

"That was the plan!" I said, and then I remembered. "Oh, you know who else knew? Mr. Avery."

"Randolph Avery? What in the world? How?"

"I'll tell you later," I said. "Actually, do you think it would be weird if I talked to his sister?"

"Yes, sweetie. Really, deeply, truly weird. Not good. She is very, very, very old."

"It's just . . . I need to look for something in that house. It's mine. You know, from that summer? It's my backpack. He kept it for me after he found out about the posters. I want to see if it's still there."

"That's just the worst idea I've ever heard, Frankie. My god, are you okay?"

"I think I'm gonna go over there," I said. "I don't think I can stop myself. I need to find it."

"Frankie? I am begging you not to go over there. This is insane. Plus, she has a live-in nurse, who is there all the time. Okay, now, remember how I said that you weren't responsible for the deaths of all those people? And, okay, Frankie, it's probably—if you work out to encompass the whole world—it's probably a lot of people who died. And *that is not on you*! But, if you kill Ms. Avery because you're trying to get some backpack from twenty years ago, then that *will* be your fault."

"Okay, I understa—"

"And what does it matter? You said the lady already knows. She's gonna write the article, right? What does it matter if you get that backpack?"

"I don't know . . . ," I said, but I kind of knew, really very strongly knew. I wanted more proof. If I was going to take credit for it, I wanted more evidence. It was a strange thing, to have hidden it for so long, and now I was starting to get paranoid that no one would really believe me.

"Okay," I said. "I'm sorry." But really I was thinking that maybe I could get Mazzy to visit with Ms. Avery, and maybe she could get the backpack. I had to calm myself down. I'd so quickly gone from terror over being discovered to intense anxiety that it would all make me look like an idiot, a fake. I decided I wanted some of those Little Debbie snack cakes, and my mom brought over two boxes, Star Crunch and Oatmeal Creme Pies, and I ate two of each very quickly, and for some reason this made my mom smile.

"You always loved junk," she said, "Pop-Tarts and Zingers and Little Debbie."

"Well, the house was full of it," I said.

"And now you barely let Junie have any," she said.

"If Junie ate a Zinger," I said, "she would shoot into the air and explode like a firework. She would destroy Bowling Green like she was Godzilla."

"Sweetie?" she asked me. The snack cakes had calmed me down, forced me to breathe, to chew, and it felt like I was sixteen again, sitting in our living room. When I looked at her, she said, "What about Zeke?"

"I don't know," I admitted. "I have to find him. I have to tell him."

I'd been putting this off for so long, didn't know what to say, how much to say. As soon as I got to college, got my first email account, the first time I'd really been able to surf the internet on my own, I looked for him. But I didn't know his name. I knew his middle name was Zeke, but it was something he was trying out for the summer, or at least that's what he had told me. I had no idea if he would still be using that name or, if he was trying to erase all evidence of that summer in Coalfield, if he was going by his first name, which I had never asked for and he had never told me. I sometimes wondered if I'd even misremembered his last name, if it was indeed Brown. And the internet wasn't as all-knowing back then, so typing in *Zeke Brown* and *Memphis* was not going to get you very far.

But I kept checking, every few months, first on AltaVista and Excite and Yahoo!, then on Google, and I'd click through the results, but there just wasn't anything there. I got on Friendster and then MySpace and then Facebook, though I never maintained any actual social media, still didn't even use Twitter or Instagram, because I didn't really want to use them and I didn't really need to use them. But I'd search for him. Nothing, or nothing that, after just a little more digging, was really him. There was a point, after I'd published the first book, when I had money and I thought I could hire a detective, but it felt wrong, like if Zeke wanted me to find him, he wouldn't make it so that I needed to involve other people.

Eventually, just searching for Ezekiel Brown finally let me hit some actual possibilities. There was a Benjamin Ezekiel Brown, born in the same year as Zeke, and Memphis had been listed in some pay-to-play sites that offered arrest records and felt very much like a scam. He might have been in Knoxville for a little while. I sometimes found hits connected to an address in North Carolina. But nothing I could pin down. Ben Brown was not an easy name to search. When his grandmother died after she moved into a nursing home in Nashville, I didn't know until months later, after visiting my mom, and no newspaper even had an obituary for her. I gave up. Or, no, I always searched, but then I stopped when it felt like that next step was necessary, to actually reach out, to call a random number and hope it was him. To hear his voice as an adult, to hear something in it that let me know it was Zeke, I couldn't make myself do it. I was waiting for him to tell me that he was ready to talk. But he never wanted to talk, I guess. He never wanted me to find him. And now I had to. Because, if I told Mazzy everything, someone would find him. And it felt so cruel to do that to him, to have someone else tell him that they knew the secret. It had to be me, no one else in the world but me.

THE NEXT AFTERNOON, I SET MYSELF UP IN MY CHILDHOOD BEDroom, which my mom had turned into a showroom for her sneakers, all these IKEA wall shelves, these shoes in neon green and void-of-space black and the kind of white that would instantly smudge if you applied even the slightest pressure from your fingertip. In the closet, I looked at the baseboard, this little opening, and there was one of my folded-up posters stuffed in there, the paper yellowed, and I let it stay there, a magical protection for my mom.

I knew that I could try harder to find Zeke, but I wouldn't hire someone, couldn't imagine trying to explain it to a detective who was wondering if I was a stalker ex-girlfriend, wanting to simply tell me that I didn't need to create some story about outsider art and satanic panic and the spirit of true collaboration. He would just need a cool grand, and then I could go kill this guy or whatever.

And so for five straight hours, I really tried, wrote down every bit of information that the internet would give me, even about people who clearly weren't Zeke, like someone from Georgia who had died in 1982, just in case it could lead me to him. I bookmarked and saved and copied and pasted, checked the distance from Coalfield to places like Eastland Heights, Georgia, and Bluffton, South Carolina, and Medford, Oregon, praying to find a single image of that goofy boy. I went to the forums devoted to the poster, where I was registered but had never commented, and searched for the name "Zeke," but nothing came up just like it hadn't come up the hundred other times I checked. I looked up Memphis and violin and art school and Cydney Hudson, his mother's maiden name, but there was nothing new, nothing that got me closer to him. I didn't even have a photo of him from that summer, hadn't even thought about it, or maybe I had assumed there would be more time, and all I could do now was try to keep the image of him in my mind, to not let time degrade it or change it. I felt like I'd done a fairly good job, could still see him so clearly, but who knows how close it was to the real thing. The entire summer still felt hallucinatory, a fairy tale, and so maybe I'd misremembered every detail about him. I mean, it took me a long time to even figure out his full name. How could I be sure what his teeth looked like? But I did. I knew that I had it right.

When I was done, I had three locations that seemed feasible, all of them ones I'd seen before, and six different phone numbers. Not a single photo. No idea about jobs or schools or if he was married or had kids. This was the edge. I was at the edge, and I had to go beyond it if I wanted him.

After I talked to Junie on the phone for about twenty minutes regarding a rare doll that she found for three hundred dollars on eBay, and after I talked to my husband about making sure that Junie did not guilt him into buying the doll, which had green face paint dripping from her eyes and was outfitted with a Technicolor dream coat, I sat in my old room and squinted until my head hurt. I took several deep breaths until I felt dizzy, and then I called the first number on the list, a Knoxville area code. I almost started crying when it rang, and then I made a little sound like a bark when it rang the second time, and then I don't remember the third or fourth or fifth ring, but then it was an answering machine recording that said, "This is Lydia, leave a message and *maybe* I'll call you back," and I just sat there, dumbfounded. There was the beep, and I was not breathing, not making a sound. I almost said the line, almost, but then I just hung up. I crossed off the number with a pen. I wanted to strangle Lydia. I was just about to try the next number when my phone rang, and I dropped the phone, then cursed, then picked it up.

"Hello," I said.

"You just called me," Lydia said, not a question but a statement of fact. Her voice had none of the sultry playfulness of the answering machine message.

"Did I?" I asked.

"Yeah," she said, "you did. Or someone at this number did. Caller ID."

"Oh, yes, I did," I said. "I realized it was the wrong number when I heard your message."

"What did you want?" she asked.

"Hmm?"

"Why did you call me?" she asked.

"Oh, ha, well, I was trying to call someone else."

"How did you get the number?" she asked. Damn, Lydia was relentless.

"I didn't. I mean, I must have misdialed. You know? Like . . . a wrong number."

"Okay then," she said, and it sounded like she did not believe me.

"Well . . . ," I said, because I needed to be sure, just so I never had to call Lydia again.

"Yeah?"

"Is there a Zeke that lives there? Or a Ben?"

"Zeke and Ben?" she asked, sounding so wary of me. Why didn't she just hang up the phone, for crying out loud?

"It's the same person. They might go by Zeke or they might go by Ben. Or Benjamin, I guess."

"No, there isn't a Ben or a Zeke or a Benjamin or anyone like that here," she said. "It's just me."

"Okay, well, sorry about that."

"Who gave you the number?" she asked.

"Lydia? What's going on? No one did. I must have misdialed. So sorry."

"What's your name?" she asked, but I hung up. My cell rang again and I declined the call and then blocked the number. It could not have gone worse. Well, no, I guess it could have been Zeke and he could have told me to go jump off a cliff. But at least then I wouldn't have had to make another phone call.

After a few minutes of pacing, of looking at my mom's sneakers, I went to the next number, a 919 area code, North Carolina, and heard a voicemail message that wasn't Zeke. I tried the Oregon number. Nothing. I tried the Georgia number and a boy told me that I had the wrong number. I tried a few that didn't even seem plausible and got the same results. And I was out of numbers.

And there was this little moment, a moment I never allowed myself, when I imagined that Zeke might be dead, that he was gone, and it didn't matter how long I searched for him. It was such a brief little window, where he went from missing to dead, and then I brought him back, that boy at the pool, his busted lip, eating that watermelon, because that was the whole point. Even if it was just in my mind, I needed Zeke to exist in order to keep going.

I looked up his mother's name, not her maiden name but as Cydney Brown, in Memphis, and found it easily, a number I had seen many times, but I had never wanted to talk to her because I didn't want that barrier between me and Zeke. It had always seemed like fate would bring Zeke into my world, but it had not. And now I needed him. I dialed the number.

It rang once and then Zeke answered. It was him, I knew immediately. Not the voice I remembered, but it was him. Why was it this easy? Why hadn't I tried this years ago? And then I felt so sick, the whole summer rushing back, and I knew exactly why I hadn't tried before.

"Hello?" he said.

"Zeke?" I asked, so shocked to hear him.

"Hello?" he said again, confused. "Who is this?"

"Zeke, it's—"

"Frankie?" he asked.

"Yeah," I replied, and I was crying. It had been so long, and just hearing him say my name, I felt the whole world stop for a second. I couldn't breathe.

"What are you doing?" he asked. "Why are you calling me? What's going on?"

"Zeke," I said, but I still couldn't get a breath. My chest was so tight. I thought I might be having a heart attack, but it was just a panic attack. It was just my entire life cracking open.

"Why would you do this, Frankie?" he asked. I heard another voice over the phone, an older woman, and she asked, "What's going on?" and he said, "It's Frankie, Mom."

"Hang up," she told him.

"I have to go," he said, but I could still hear him breathing. I was trying so hard not to say it.

"Frankie," he said, "are you still there?"

I hung up the phone.

I tossed it away from me, pulled my knees up to my chest, holding myself steady. You know what I was saying to myself, right? I was saying it. Again and again. I waited for the phone to ring, for Zeke to come find me, now that I'd found him. But the phone was so quiet. The house was so quiet.

I held on to myself, my eyes closed. I saw the poster in my mind, those hands reaching out. I didn't know who the hands belonged to. Were they mine? I hoped not. I rocked and rocked. I prayed that my mom would not come check on me. I had no idea if anything else in the world still existed. My room went back to the way it was, my dumb posters and dirty laundry, candy wrappers everywhere, and I was a teenager, the summer heat making everything wavy, just before I met Zeke for the first time. And I let myself live in that temporary space, before anything had happened. And it felt so good, and I wondered why I'd stayed alive, why I ever left that moment.

I fell asleep, and when I woke up, at four in the morning, I checked my phone. I was back in the real world. Zeke was gone again.

But I'd found him. He couldn't disappear. I had his number. I had the address. I just had to dial the number again. I could call forever, hitting redial, over and over and over, until I pulled him back into the world that we'd made together. I wondered what he was doing right now, what he must have been thinking. He lived with his mom, maybe. Or she lived with him. I wasn't sure.

He had no idea about Mazzy Brower, or the article, or that I had admitted to making the poster. He only knew that the girl from the summer when he maybe had ruined his entire life had called him out of the blue. I knew it was a surprise to him. It had to be. I had been the one trying to find *him*, had prepared myself for it, and when I heard his voice, I lost my mind. I hoped he was okay. I hoped he knew I wasn't trying to hurt him, but how in the world would he know that? Maybe he needed to be very afraid of me.

And there was really only one way to find out. It was still dark outside, but I packed up my stuff and left a note for my mom, saying where I was going and that I would call her in the morning, that I'd bring Junie to see her soon. Then I was in the car, driving, on my way to Zeke, the edge, the edge, the edge, the edge.

Sixteen

I WAS TWO HOURS INTO THE FOUR-AND-A-HALF-HOUR DRIVE when my mom called me. "Frankie!" she said. "Jesus, why didn't you wait until the morning? I walked into your room, and it was like you'd ascended into heaven. It was very unsettling."

"I left you a note, Mom," I said, trying to stay awake, grateful for the distraction, even one this awkward.

"You left the note in your bedroom, sweetie," she replied. "So I didn't *get* the note until *after* I thought you'd been kidnapped. You leave the note in *my* bedroom or in the kitchen, okay? Like, in the future, you leave the note somewhere accessible."

"I'm sorry, Mom," I said. "I wasn't in the best frame of mind."

"So you decided to drive to Memphis in that frame of mind? Sweetie, this feels like that summer all over again.

You're in the car, and you are alone, and . . . just be careful. I wish you'd let me come with you. I kind of thought it might be like a road trip or something for us."

"I just think I need to do this, so I can move on to whatever is next."

"Your life? Right? The rest of your life with your husband and your daughter? When you say something, sweetie, like *whatever is next*, it is not reassuring, okay?"

"Mom! Jesus, of course, I mean the rest of my life. My whole life. Just getting back to Bowling Green and being with Aaron and Junie and writing my books and, I don't know, being outed as a freak who caused a national panic."

"Could you, at the very least, text me the address where you're going? So I can give it to the police if you disappear? So I can drive there? Wait, if I left right now—"

"Mom! It's okay. I'm okay. I need to do this. I'll text you that address so you have it."

"It's Zeke?" she asked. "You're sure it's him?"

"Yes, it's him. I'm going to go see him. I'll tell him, let him know that this is happening, and then I'll go home."

"Okay," she said. "If I didn't stop you back then, I don't know what I can do about it now. None of us really has the moral high ground, I guess I'm saying. Please, please, please be careful. Do you have pepper spray?"

"No, I don't. I don't need pepper spray."

"I have twenty of them in the kitchen. I wish you would have taken one."

"I don't want it. Not to talk to Zeke. I'd better go. I've got to get some gas at the next exit."

"Sweetie?" she said. "Would it even matter to tell him? You haven't seen him in forever. You don't know him. Not really. Just tell the reporter that Zeke helped you and then things will happen naturally after that. Maybe it's better if that lady talks to him. It might be better, honestly."

"I already called him. He heard my voice. I just need to tell him."

"I wish you wouldn't, but okay. I really feel like I should come with you. If you waited at a rest stop, I—"

"I gotta go, Mom," I said. "I'll be okay. I'll text you the address. I'll text you when I'm done. It's fine."

I got out of the car once I pulled into a gas station, and bought some Pop-Tarts and a soda. The station was empty, just the cashier, who was watching TV, and so I walked to the car and got one of the posters, some tape, and I went back into the store and slipped into the women's bathroom. I taped it to the mirror and stared at it for ten seconds, letting it wash over me. Why did it work every time? Why did I care so much? I didn't question it. Or I didn't question it more deeply. I let it do its thing to me, the world disappearing and then wrapping around me. And then I was gone.

•

IN MEMPHIS, THE ADDRESS LED ME TO THAT SAME HOUSE FROM the summer, the cottage in Central Gardens. I had been hoping that it wouldn't be the same house, since the last time I was here, there had been some weird violence, a lot of chaos. I didn't even consider driving away, but I thought about Zeke, that goofy teenage boy, and how those fits of anger would spark, and I was scared. I wished that I weren't, but I was.

And then, before I even got out of the car, Zeke was standing on the porch, staring at me. After twenty years, of course someone looks different, but really I was just softer, a little heavier, and my skin was clearer. It was still me, and if you saw me as a teenager, nothing would throw you when you looked at me now. Zeke was so lean, muscle and bone, like someone who ran marathons or climbed mountains. He had grown into his features and now looked kind of handsome instead of goofy, which saddened me a little, honestly. He looked like he was one of two things: a man who made coffee tables from reclaimed driftwood and sold them for three grand, or a man who was very, very suspicious of the circumstances of 9/11. I guess I'd thought, and it was stupid to think this, that Zeke would still be a teenager, that he'd look like how I remembered him. And it made it harder to get out of the car, to walk toward him, when he seemed like someone I didn't recognize. I waved to him, or I held up my hand, and he nodded, like he'd been expecting me but had hoped I wouldn't come.

"Hey," I said after I rolled down the window.

He looked at me for a few seconds; I saw the flash of fear cross his face, but then he finally relaxed his posture. "Hey," he finally said. "Hey, Frankie."

"It's been a really long time since I last saw you," I said, and I wondered how it was possible for every single thing you said to sound so dumb, so weightless. I wanted to say, "I missed you," but it wasn't really true, I was now realizing. I missed teenage Zeke. This guy was a stranger. He was the person I had to talk to in order to get Zeke back. I got out of the car and walked over to him.

"It's been twenty-one years," he said. The last time I had been this close to him, my arm had been snapped nearly in half, my mouth bleeding, my whole world ruined. I could feel my heart beating so fast.

"Do you still go by Zeke or did you change it back or—"

"I go by Ben," he said.

"It's going to be really hard for me to call you that," I admitted.

"It doesn't matter," he admitted, looking so sheepish. "You can call me whatever."

"Can I come talk to you?" I asked. "It's important."

Just then, Zeke's mom came onto the porch. She wasn't smiling, but she didn't look angry. She touched Zeke's shoulder and he turned to look at her. And then, holy shit, his dad came out, walking with a cane, and asked Zeke if he was okay. I could not believe that they were still married. Or maybe they weren't. Why was Zeke still living with them? I guessed I needed to get inside and maybe I'd find out. I did not like that the fact of his parents staying together was overwhelming my focus on Zeke. I waited for permission, because I wouldn't come in if Zeke said no. I mean, I would later throw a rock through their window with a message that explained everything, but I would not go into their house without Zeke's okay.

He took a deep breath, looked back at his parents, and then nodded. "Yeah, come on in," he said.

"You were hard to find, honestly," I said, still not moving, and he smiled for just a flash of a second, and I saw those weird teeth and it instantly made me happy, calmed me down, even though he went back to his deadpan look right after.

"I mean, kind of?" he said. "I'm in the house where I grew up. I didn't leave."

"Well, okay, but it was hard to find you *online*."

"Yeah, okay."

"Did you not want people to find you?" I asked.

"*No one* is trying to find me," he said, smiling again. "Except, you know, for you."

"Well," I said, "I found you."

"You did."

"Honey, maybe we can go inside?" his mom said, looking around as if a crowd were on the sidewalk watching us. "Hello, Frankie," she said to me.

"Hi, Mrs. . . . well, hello. And, hello, Mr. Brown. I don't know if you remember m—"

And the whole family laughed, a real laugh, over something so strange as the fact that I'd kicked him so freaking hard in the knee while his son had tried to murder him.

"I do remember you," Mr. Brown said. "Very well."

I looked at his cane, my eyes so wide, and he shook his head. "This was all later," he admitted. "A stroke."

"Oh," I said, "good. I mean, not, you know, not good that you had . . . You look well, sir." I turned back to Zeke. "Do you know why I'm here?" I asked. "Like, can you guess?"

"Jeez, Frankie, yeah, I can guess. Here, just . . . come inside."

The whole family kind of awkwardly shuffled back into the house, and there was this moment when I realized that I could walk inside and Zeke and his parents could stuff me in a hidden room and the secret would stay a secret. But then I remembered my mom, all those cans of pepper spray, this address on her phone, and I knew I was safe.

"Frankie, would you like some coffee? A muffin?" his mom asked. This was the first time that his mother had ever talked to me.

"I'm okay," I said. "I drank a Mountain Dew and ate some Pop-Tarts on the way here."

"Pop-Tarts," Zeke repeated, like he was slowly remembering me, like he had amnesia and my presence was bringing it all back. There was still something off about him, the delayed way he seemed to respond to me, but I felt like that was warranted. I had not seen him in so long and now here I was. All that time I'd dreamed of bringing him back, and he was right here. All that time I'd dreamed of bringing him back, I guess I'd never thought about how, really, it would be me returning to him, making myself known. It was all very weird. And that was comforting, as if weirdness was the thread that connected us, all we really knew of each other, the way we made each other feel like the rest of the world wasn't real.

"Ben, should we leave you alone, or do you want us to stay?" Mr. Brown asked his son.

"Maybe . . . I think maybe we can be alone. I'll let you know if I need you," Zeke said.

"Or," Zeke's mom said, "maybe we should talk to Frankie first?" She nodded to her husband. "We could talk to her and see why she's here and then we could tell you about it."

That sounded utterly miserable to me, just so painful, and I prayed that Zeke would not do this. I didn't want a chaperone. We had always been left alone. Although, shit, that had maybe not been a good idea.

"No," Zeke replied, "it's okay. We'll talk."

"Well . . . we'll just be in the kitchen," Mr. Brown said, smiling at me.

"Eating muffins and drinking coffee," Zeke's mom added.

"What kind of muffins?" I asked.

"Banana," she answered immediately. "Are you sure you don't want one?"

"No," I replied. "I don't know why I even asked. I'm . . . I was just curious."

"Banana," Zeke's mom said again, nodding, sure of herself.

After they left, Zeke gestured to the couch, and I sat down, and it was a really soft couch. I kind of sank into it, and my feet weren't touching the floor, and Zeke sat on an orange leather chair that supported him perfectly. I tried to get resettled but the sofa kept kind of pulling my ass farther into the cushions. Maybe it was a sofa bed? I'm not sure. It was a bad position to be in, not the kind of furniture you want for this kind of reunion.

"So—" I started to say, but of course that was the exact moment that Zeke started talking.

"I read your book," he said.

"Oh, wow," I replied.

"I liked it. I've read all of them. They're really good. I think I like the first one the best, because I remember you writing it."

"I guess I kind of hoped you might read it," I said.

"I did," he said. He paused. "And you're married, right? You have a kid. I promise I haven't been searching for you. I . . . just . . . that's what the bio on the book said."

"No, it's okay. I mean. I searched for you online, so it's fine. I am married. And I have a little girl. Just one. Junie."

He nodded, like this all checked out.

"And do you have . . . are you . . . like . . ." I didn't know what to ask. He was in his childhood home. What was his life? Why was I so weird? I wanted this. I wanted to know, but now it felt so strange, to be close to him and realize how much time had passed.

"No, no, I am *not* married," he said. "And no kids. No."

"Oh, okay," I said.

"I have a girlfriend," he offered. "I mean, I've had a few of them, but I have one right now. Nita. She's a teacher. She's nice."

"That's great, Zeke."

"Yeah," he said.

I was just about to ask him about work when he cut in.

"I do live here with my mom and dad," he said. "I mean, I haven't always. I've lived in some other places, too. I went to art school. I moved around a little. But . . . I don't know. I had some problems. I guess I still have them."

"It's okay, Zeke," I said. He looked so embarrassed, and it hurt me that he would think I'd judge him.

"I got diagnosed as bipolar, but that took a while. At first, they thought it might be something else. It took a long time to get it all figured out. Hospitals? The medication, you know? A lot of different ones because some of them were bad. And I'd go somewhere and get settled but then something would happen or I wouldn't feel right, and I'd come back here. So I just stay here now. It's good for me. All my doctors are here. It's familiar to me."

"That's good," I offered. "And your mom and dad are . . . like . . . they're still together?"

He laughed, which made me so happy. "Yeah, they are. It's weird, but when we came back to Memphis, my dad kind of realized he had been awful to us. He felt so bad. And he shaped up. He helped take care of me. And they really do love each other, I think. I'm around them a lot, so I think I'd know. It's better than . . . well, better than before."

"What do you do? Or, like, do you work? Or, like . . ."

"I do art stuff," he said. "I ink for different comic book companies."

"Wait, what?" I said. "Oh, that's really cool, Zeke."

"I ink a lot for Marvel. I used to ink for DC. I'm not, like, quite what they would want for art, but mostly I realized that I'm really good with lines, you know? I'm good at going over someone's work and making it better. And it's good for me, to kind of have something already there for me to work with so I don't get too carried away."

"I didn't see your work online," I said. I wanted to search right now on my phone, but I kept staring at him, trying so hard to reconcile the Zeke I remembered with the person in front of me. The more I heard his voice, the easier it was.

"I go by my initials," he said. "Like a tag? It's BEB. But, like, even then you aren't going to see much of me online. Like, inking is not super sexy. It's not something people write about." He paused for a few seconds, looking right at me. "But I am good at it. I know that."

"I bet," I said, thinking, of course, of course, of the poster, those lines.

I'd almost forgotten why I'd come; I was so struck by being this near to him, how weird time felt to me in this moment. And I knew that in some way, what I was going to say would ruin it.

"Zeke, it's just—"

"I want to say that I'm sorry," Zeke suddenly said, his voice rising just a bit, cracking. He kept interrupting me just as I was going to say the thing I needed to say, like he was afraid of what it would be. "I'm really sorry, Frankie."

"What?" I replied.

"That I hurt you," he said. "More than once, you know? I did that awful thing to you in the car, after my dad, when you were trying to help me. I messed up so bad. I'm sorry that I hurt you on the porch, and even worse, that I didn't help you and that I left and that I never talked to you again. Things were just really bad for me. And then time passed, you know? It kept going and going, and I kept trying to get away from that summer, because it had ruined my life a little, and there was just no way for me to get back to you or apologize. And it's just been this guilt, always, and it's never left. And I'm sorry."

"It's okay," I said. I didn't want to admit how badly I had needed him to say all this. I needed him to say that he'd hurt me, had done something pretty bad, and then I could say that I'd survived it. I thought about reaching for him, but of course

I didn't. "Zeke, you didn't hurt me. Or, like, yeah, my arm, whatever, but I'm okay."

"Are you?" he asked, and I could see a little panic move across his features. "Like, you're here, right? Something must be wrong."

"Not . . . wrong, exactly. It's just . . . Zeke, the thing is, a reporter found out that it was me. She knows I made the poster—"

"Oh," he said, shaking his head.

"—but it's okay. I told her that I did it. I'm just . . . I'm ready to admit it. And she's going to write this article about it, and she's going to interview me. It's all going to come out."

"Shit, Frankie," he said, still shaking his head. "How did she find out?"

"It's so complicated. I'll tell you, but, just, right now, I wanted to let you know. It's going to come out. People are going to know."

"Did you tell this reporter about me?" he asked.

"I haven't," I admitted. "Not a word, I promise."

"But you're going to tell her?" he asked.

"Shouldn't I? Like, you made it, too. We made it, you and me."

"But, you haven't told her?" he asked, like he'd found some loophole that he could exploit, the way he leaned forward to look more closely at me. "She doesn't know?"

"Not yet. That's what I'm saying, Zeke. I wanted to let you know before I told her."

There was a long pause. I had to keep scooting a little bit at a time to keep from sinking into the sofa.

"I'm scared, Frankie," he finally said.

"Me, too," I told him. "But I don't know what else to do. I just . . . I think I need to admit it. I feel like I have to say it was me and just kind of see what happens."

"Frankie?" he asked.

"Yeah?"

"Could you not tell this reporter about me?" he asked. "Like, just tell her that you did it by yourself?"

"I . . . no, why would—"

"I'm scared. You're a famous writer, and you can admit it, and it might be interesting to see what happens, but I think I know what will happen to me. I think it will do bad things to me."

"But, maybe not?" I offered, and it felt so lame. It felt cruel. But I couldn't stop. "Because it won't just be you, right? I'll say that we did it. You and me. And I think maybe I can take whatever scares you and I can handle it."

"I don't think so, Frankie," he said.

"I just . . . I can't imagine it not being the two of us," I told him.

"It was so long ago," he said.

"It doesn't feel like that long ago to me, honestly," I told him. "I think about it all the time. I think about that summer. I say the phrase to myself. If I'm just sitting by myself, not really thinking about anything, I see those hands that you drew, just kind of hovering there in my mind. You don't have that?"

"No," he admitted, and he looked so sheepish, so sad. But I think he was sad for *me*. "I work hard not to think about it. And I don't."

"That summer is why I'm who I am," I said.

"Me, too," he told me.

I had thought I was going to bring Zeke back, and I had thought he'd be grateful, once the shock wore off. We'd be friends again. Or at least when people thought of the poster, they'd think of us that summer, the two of us, and even if we never saw each other again, we'd be linked. I wanted to cry.

"It was our secret," he said. "We said we'd never tell. It was just you and me. And I really did like that, Frankie."

"I have to tell," I said. "It's happening, whether or not I tell."

"But, couldn't it still be our secret?" he asked. "You can tell them a story. You can tell them that it was you. And that will be the truth. And people will believe it. From here on out, even after we die, that will be the story of that summer. And it will just be you and me who still know what the truth is."

"I think I'm a little scared to do it by myself," I said. "I don't think I would have done any of it that summer if I hadn't met you. I feel . . . Zeke, I feel like you made me the person that I am. I'm really grateful for that."

"I like that," he said.

"But did I make you the person that you are?" I asked him.

"Yes. You did. Or we both did. Or the world did. I don't know. But it's not bad. I'm not sad about it," he said.

"I wish you hadn't gone away," I told him. "I wish that summer had never ended." When I said it out loud, I realized how childish it sounded, how self-absorbed. I didn't exactly wish that Zeke had stayed, I now understood. I wanted us to be frozen in that moment, for time to have stopped moving forward.

"It's hard to imagine what would have happened if I stayed," he replied. "I would have liked to see you again. But I think I needed to go. I think that summer was all we could have."

Whether or not it was psychotic, whether it meant that I had deep-seated issues and had fixated so heavily on a single summer that my whole life was wrapped around it, I didn't care. I needed it. I would never disown it. It was mine.

I looked at Zeke, that beautiful boy. And I realized that this was Ben. This was Ben and he wasn't a kid. And I remembered that, before that one summer, he was also Ben. And he'd made a whole life without me. That thing we'd created together. I guess it was mine alone now.

"Okay," I finally said. "I'll say I did all of it."

"Thank you," Zeke said.

It was not how I had expected it to go, or maybe it was not how I had *dreamed* it might go. I don't know exactly what I had hoped. You hold on to something for twenty years, the expectations and possibilities bend and twist alongside your actual life. I knew I didn't want him to be in love with me. I didn't want to run away with him, to completely undo the life I'd spent so long making, the life that I truly loved. I guess I'd hoped that we'd say the phrase together, maybe a hundred times? Maybe a thousand? I feel like if we'd sat on the porch swing and repeated the line a thousand times, it would have satisfied me, but who knows? Maybe after all that, hours later, I would have said, "Maybe another thousand times?" But I could see now that if I even asked him to say it one time, to even say *the edge*, he might turn into smoke. But here's the thing. I was going to do just what he asked. So I needed something. And because I hadn't anticipated this, I didn't know what to ask for.

Zeke went to get us a muffin, and then he sat on the sofa with me while we ate. We talked about what came after that summer, the immediate aftermath. I told him about the car crash, about Randolph Avery (and how his letters had given it all away), and my broken arm and that year after. I told him about Hobart and my mom falling in love and then him dying. I told him about the school where I ended up going, about leaving Coalfield for the first time really. And falling in love with Aaron, and writing my books, and having Junie.

He told me about art school, about running, which he said was good to combat the weight he'd gain from the medications, but it also sometimes became so obsessive that it was worse for him than his freakouts. It was a fine line, he said, how deeply he let himself become obsessed with something, learning when to pull back. He ran only two marathons a year, no more and no less. That was the sweet spot. He talked about the squirrels in the park near his house, how he could get them to climb into his lap and sit with him. He seemed happy, and I was overjoyed, sincerely, to know this. I hadn't ruined him. He hadn't ruined me. We'd stayed alive in this world. I didn't want that to change.

I liked hearing Zeke talk, could hear that specific timbre of his voice, the way it got a little squeaky, and I was happy to see his teeth, his nervous tics, but it was hard to believe from our normal conversation that we were the two people who had made that poster.

I wanted to tell him how I still had the original poster, our blood on it. I wanted to say how I'd put up a poster in pretty much every town I'd ever visited. I wanted to tell him that so much of my brain was filled with the specific details of that summer, how much he lived inside of me. But I didn't want to make him anxious. I didn't want to hurt him. Really and truly, I didn't. I didn't need him to do another blood pact. Did I want it? I did. I wanted it just so that I could feel that thread that connected me to the past. Is that why we do anything in this life? To feel it vibrate along the line that starts at birth and ends way way way after we die? I didn't know. And I wasn't going to figure it out in his childhood home, sleep-deprived, wrung out, a fugitive. What could I ask him? What could he give me?

"Zeke?" I finally said.

"Yeah, Frankie?" he replied.

"Could you do something for me?"

"Do you want me to say it?" he guessed. "You want me to say the phrase?"

"I don't know. I did. But I honestly think it might be bad. You have to teach me how to draw it."

"The poster?" he asked.

I nodded. "If I say I made it, then I have to draw it."

"Have you not tried before?" he asked, confused. "You seem, you know, pretty obsessed with it. You never tried to draw it yourself?"

"Why would I?" I asked him. "I wrote the line. You drew the picture. That's how it worked."

"Okay," he said. "I think I can do this. Here, come to my room." He turned to the kitchen. "Mom? Dad? I'm taking Frankie to my room."

"Okay," they said in unison, and their ease made me think that they had dealt with much worse. I mean, I had been responsible for much worse, but I was still grateful that they let us go into his room.

His room was crazy neat, and the walls were covered with framed pages of old comic books.

"It's, like, the one thing I spend money on," he admitted. "These are original works by guys like Wally Wood and Johnny Craig."

"They're really cool," I said.

He had a desk with some of his projects stacked up, but he moved them out of the way. I got out my phone and pulled up a picture of the poster. He looked at it for a second, like he was admiring the work of one of those pages on his walls. Like he hadn't made it. He kind of smiled, and then he nodded. He got out some paper and pens. "Okay, yeah," he said. I was a little shocked that it didn't unsettle him more; I wondered how long it had been since he'd last seen it. I wondered if ever, in his whole life, he had seen one of the posters that I had hung up after that summer.

I took a pen and wrote the phrase, just like before. I took another blank page and did the same thing. It looked exactly like the original. It was so easy to do.

"Now show me," I told him.

It was such a relief when he eased up, gave in. He stared at the page. I saw him reading the phrase, remembering the rhythm, like a prayer. And then he started drawing those lines, so delicate and yet a little rough, primitive, the way he bore down sometimes without meaning to, and I copied him as best I could. After about twenty minutes, constantly looking back at the poster for guidance, he had most of it sketched out. I loved watching his hands, the way he seemed, with each new consideration, to wave his fingertips across what I'd written, like he was reminding himself of its presence on the page.

"The buildings," he told me, looking at mine, "are too small. You need to, like, connect them, but make them bigger. And, like, here, make the windows like this, just—" and he leaned over me and showed me on my own page. I copied him, feeling the image come together the way I'd hoped it would.

The beds were harder, the children, and I kind of messed it up, but I mostly focused on him, watching where he started each new line. I wished he'd have let me video the process, so I could go back and see exactly where he set his pen, but I was already committing it to memory. I was good at this, I think, knowing when I needed to remember something for later.

He did the hands last, and I followed along, and they looked close enough. I knew I'd practice. I'd make it a thousand times before I showed it to Mazzy, if she even asked. She knew something was complicated about the poster, that someone else was involved, and I would have to say that I'd copied it from someone, someone from years before, or I'd say that I found it in an old book, or that I found it in our house, or something. I could figure out that part.

When he was done, he took a deep breath, really considered the drawing. "This feels so weird," he admitted. "I don't draw like this anymore. I like it."

"Could you do it again?" I asked.

"Again?" he replied, looking at me.

"One more time," I told him.

"Okay, sure. One more," he said, and started again.

I didn't even try to copy him. I just watched him draw.

And then he was done. I took it and put it with the other one. I nodded. "Okay," I said, but he got another piece of paper. And he started to draw.

After about ten minutes, he had sketched this forest, these trees, stripped of leaves, the limbs thin and sharp. And then he drew a clearing in the middle, just enough space to suggest an opening. And then he stopped. He looked at me, and I nodded. It was good. *Keep going.*

And he drew this little house, like a fairy-tale cottage. I was about to tell him that I thought it was enough, that I liked it, but then, all around the house, on the floor of the forest, he drew what at first I thought were brambles. But he kept building and building and building, and I realized that they were flames, a fire, and it wound around the cottage, but not so near that it would harm the cottage, and not so far that it would burn down the forest. It was this circle of flame, properly demarcating the world, what was inside and what was outside.

"Do you want this one?" he asked when he was done.

"Yeah," I said. I'd take all of it. I would take anything.

And we sat there in his room, the house humming. I knew I needed to leave soon, to get back to my life, to let him stay inside of his own. But it was hard to leave.

And it was like Zeke knew that I was having trouble figuring out how to do this, to walk away.

"Maybe I'll see you again?" he asked. "Maybe later? After all this happens?"

"If you want to," I offered.

"Let me see how I feel once it comes out. I'll need to figure it out. Watch myself."

"Sure, of course," I replied. I didn't think it would happen, and that was okay, honestly. I would not ask for more.

And then Zeke said it, the line. He remembered it. He hadn't forgotten. How could he? And then we said it together.

"Goodbye, Zeke," I finally said.

"Goodbye, Frankie," he said.

He walked me to the porch, and I said goodbye to his parents.

I took the posters, and I went back to my car. I didn't look back at him. I pulled out of the driveway. I could not remember when I had last slept. Everything was a dream. I would never sleep again, maybe. I drove back to my home, back to a place that was familiar to me. I hoped so badly that it would be familiar to me. I needed it. And the miles ticked off, my car taking me there, and I promised myself that it would be a good place. I would make it. I'd keep making it. I said the line to myself, and it sounded so right. I had made that. I loved it.

Seventeen

WHEN I GOT HOME, JUNIE RAN OUTSIDE TO MEET ME. SHE hugged me and I smelled her, the unmistakable scent of my daughter, and I held on to her. Aaron was in the doorway. He smiled, but it was that kind of smile where you're showing just enough teeth that you're like, *I might grind my teeth to dust if you've ruined our lives*, and I gave him the kind of smile that says, *I have everything under control, you dope.* I absolutely did not. But it's such a nice smile, and he accepted it so easily.

I knew that I'd now have to talk to Mazzy Brower, and I'd have to let her really examine the poster. And I'd have to drive back to Coalfield and I would take her to all those places on the map, which I still had, and we would see how many of them were still around. And I'd tell her a version of the story that would become the truth, and I would still get to keep the real thing, what I'd made that summer, a secret.

I was keeping it for me and Zeke, but really it was for me. It was just for me.

But here was Junie in my arms, so lovely, wriggling and weird and already wanting to tell me about that doll, the demon doll that spit fire that she had to have because she had seen a picture of it in some old children's book that she had discovered at the library. And I let her tell me. I would buy her that doll. I hoped it was as hideous as I had imagined in my mind. I hoped that Junie kept it for her entire life. Aaron hugged me as we walked up to the porch. "It's okay?" he asked, and he trusted me. I know that he trusted me.

And even though the story I told Mazzy wouldn't include it, I would tell him about Zeke, about that whole summer. I'd tell him what it felt like to be alone in that little place, things I wouldn't be able to say in the article, things no one would really care about. How I never knew how I'd get to the place where I was okay. I'd tell him about that weird boy, and how I was going to hide him away, and I hoped Aaron would understand.

"It's okay," I told him. "Really. It is. I'm okay."

We went into the house, the three of us, and we left the front door wide open, completely unprotected, because nothing would hurt us. Forever and forever and forever.

THAT NIGHT, PUTTING JUNIE TO SLEEP, I LAY BESIDE HER AND WE read from a chapter book about a pack of wolves chasing these two girls on a train. And after, when I'd turned off the light, Junie said, "Where have you been?"

"To see Nana," I told her. "Remember?"

"But why?" she asked. "What's going on?"

"When I was a girl—"

"My age? My age right now?" Junie interrupted.

"Older. When I was a teenager, I made this thing. And it was a secret. And people really were wild about it, and they got crazy over it."

"Why was it a secret?" she asked. "Was it bad?"

"No," I said. "I don't think so."

"But you kept it a secret?" she asked.

"I did. For a long time. Until just now, really. And now I'm going to reveal the secret. And I guess we'll see what happens."

"What will happen?" she asked.

"I don't know. I really don't. But nothing bad. Probably something good. Something amazing."

"I hope so," she said. I could hear her breathing. "Can you tell me the secret right now?"

"I could. It's just this line. It goes: *The edge is a shantytown filled with gold seekers. We are fugitives, and the law—*"

"*—is skinny with hunger for us,*" Junie said, finishing it.

"Why do you know that?" I asked, though I kind of knew. But it was still a surprise.

"You say it all the time, Mom," she told me. "You said it when I was a baby."

"I don't think you remember being a baby, sweetie," I said.

"Well, I do," she said, defiant. "And you would say it to me at night, like . . . like a lullaby? I really do remember it."

And I had, of course. I had told her every night, the only person I could tell, and I'd whisper it to her, the words piling up, but I said them so softly, underneath the sound machine, an ocean, which filled the room. But she had remembered.

"Well, that's the secret," I said. "That's all it is."

"I like it," she said. "I like how it sounds. I like gold."

"I know, sweetie," I said. "I like gold, too."

"We are fugitives," she said.

"We are," I told her.

"You and me?" she asked.

"Yes," I told her.

"And Daddy?"

"Yes."

"And Nana? And Pop-Pop and Gigi?"

"Yes."

"And the Triplet Uncles? Uncle Marcus and Aunt Mina? And Dominic and Angie?"

"Yeah, I guess so. Yes."

"And my teachers? All the kids at my school?"

"Yes."

"And the whole world? Everyone in the world?"

"Yes, all of them."

"And everyone that has ever lived?"

"Okay, sure."

"And everyone that hasn't been born yet but will be born? Them, too? They're fugitives?"

"Well . . . yeah. Them, too."

It was dark, but there were those little glow-in-the-dark stars on her ceiling, so many of them, like, we'd really let her go crazy with the glow stars, and I stared at them, the sky above us, the universe.

"Is it good to be a fugitive?" she finally asked.

"I think so," I said. "It can be."

"Good," she finally said, and then she was fast asleep, unbothered. But I didn't get up. Not just yet, but I knew I would.

Soon I would stand up and walk into the hallway and then into our bedroom, and into my own bed, with Aaron, and then the sun would come up, and light would fill the house, and I would wake up and things would go on from there. But right now, looking up at those stars that were not stars but more like stars than the real ones to me, I lay in that bed, breathing, alive. I said the line. Nothing had changed. I said it, and every single word was exactly the same, just as I had made it that summer. It would never change. So I said it again. And again. And again.

Acknowledgments

Thanks to the following:

Julie Barer, the most important person in my writing life, who has made so much possible for me, and everyone at the Book Group, especially Nicole Cunningham.

Helen Atsma, my editor extraordinaire, who helped me understand how to tell this story, and everyone at Ecco, especially Sonya Cheuse, Meghan Deans, Miriam Parker, and Allison Saltzman. I have been so lucky to be with Ecco from the beginning, and I cannot imagine where I would be without the support of this amazing publisher and these amazing people.

Jason Richman at United Talent Agency, for his kindness and support.

The University of the South and the English and Creative Writing departments, with gratitude for the opportunity to be a part of this community.

My family: Kelly and Debbie Wilson; Kristen, Wes, and Kellan Huffman; Mary Couch; Meredith, Warren, Laura, Morgan, and Philip James; and the Wilson, Fuselier, and Baltz families.

My friends: Brian Baltz, Aaron Burch, Sonya Cheuse, Lucy Corin, Lee Conell, Lily Davenport, Marcy Dermansky, Sam Esquith, Isabel Galbraith, Elizabeth and John Grammer, Jason Griffey, Brandon Iracks-Edeline, Kate Jayroe, Gwen Kirby, Shelley MacLauren, Kelly Malone, Katie McGhee, Matt O'Keefe, Cecily Parks, Ann Patchett, Betsy Sandlin, Matt Schrader, Leah Stewart, David and Heidi Syler, Jeff Thompson, Rufi Thorpe, Lauryl Tucker, Zack Wagman, and Caki Wilkinson.

And, as always, with all my love: Leigh Anne, Griff, and Patch.